"What's the disturbance?" the sergeant asked.

"There's been a killing," Doc answered nonchalantly, gesturing toward Raider in a grand style. "My friend there, the tall, rough-looking gentleman, shot the head off that unfortunate ruffian. You'll probably find what's left of the head at the bottom of the back alley."

The younger officer ran out immediately, holding his hand over his mouth. The sergeant took a long look at the body, twirling the end of his bright orange mustache. Then he glanced at Raider, who still rested his hand on the butt of his holstered .44 . . .

J.D. HARDIN

VENGEANCE VALLEY

BERKLEY BOOKS, NEW YORK

VENGEANCE VALLEY

A Berkley Book / published by arrangement with
the author

PRINTING HISTORY
Berkley edition / August 1984

ISBN: 0-425-07114-6
A BERKLEY BOOK ® TM 757,375
Berkley Books are published by Berkley Publishing Group,
200 Madison Avenue, New York, NY 10016.
The name "BERKLEY" and the stylized "B" with design are trademarks
belonging to Berkley Publishing Corporation.

CHAPTER ONE

"I don't give two hoots in hell if I ever see Oregon again," Raider said.

Doc Weatherbee glanced toward his broad-shouldered partner, who swung like a listless tree trunk in the saddle on the gray mare. The mount was Raider's only memory of the Territorial Timber Company of Oregon, the last Pinkerton client to purchase their investigative services. A payroll thief had run them ragged through the giant redwoods and lumber camps, one step ahead of their efforts. It had taken them three weeks to nab the bandit, who had been working with the payroll clerk for the timber company. The clerk had been paying with one hand and taking it back with the other.

"It rained every miserable con-sarned day," Raider continued, casting a wary eye to the dark clouds overhead. "And I ain't never seen bugs like that. Damned mosquitoes were big enough to carry off a wolverine. I feel like I've got ticks crawling all over me."

"That's to be expected with the watershed being—"

"All I want is a hot bath and a bed," Raider said. "And maybe somebody to share it with me. I swear to the Almighty—"

"Yes, continually," Doc interrupted. "I've been listening

to you swear since before we crossed over into California. I know you're bubbling with aggravation, Raider, especially since we missed the stage and were forced to accept these hay-burning steeds. I'd be most appreciative if you'd put a lid on the cauldron."

Raider growled at Doc, who managed to sit straight on the chestnut gelding in spite of his fatigue. Still, Doc's usually dapper presence had virtually melted under the intense precipitation of the Pacific Northwest. Raider took a certain satisfaction in the drooping felt of Doc's pearl gray derby. But when Doc managed to ignite a sulphur match with the intention of torching his last Old Virginia cheroot, Raider groaned, feeling his stomach begin to tumble over and over.

"Does the smoke annoy you?" Doc asked, knowing it did.

"As sure as Satan it makes me want to puke," Raider replied.

"Good," Doc replied.

Before they had ridden another half mile on the clay road, the sky erupted again, dropping a deluge to extinguish the orange glow on the tip of Doc's cigar. Doc tucked the stogie into his slicker, ignoring the satisfied smirk that crept across Raider's grizzled countenance. Their horses splashed the muddy path as rain pelted the puddled ground like shots fired from a Gatling gun. The smirk vanished from Raider's face. He couldn't decide which he hated more, the rain or the smoke.

"I don't guess you have a notion of how far we are from Frisco," Raider said.

"My notion is that we are approximately thirty miles away," Doc replied. "However, with your incessant grumbling, it will no doubt seem like three hundred."

"This damned rain could strangle a frog," Raider said.

"Raider, when we finally reach San Francisco, will you grant me one request?"

"What's that, Doc?"

"Do your best to stay away from me for at least forty-eight hours," Doc replied.

Even in the miserable downpour, Raider thought that would be the easiest thing he had ever done.

"Where have you been, Doc? To the gates of hell?"

"Only purgatory," Doc replied. "I daresay Dante himself would not have been amused."

Doc's crumpled form swayed in the foyer of Paxton's Haberdashery of San Francisco, an exclusive shop which catered to gentlemen of distinction. Greeting him was the gentle face of Louise Paxton, the widow of the late proprietor and Doc's friend, Ronald Paxton. Ronald's last words had been for Doc to take care of Louise, a request that Doc had fulfilled in every degree.

"I just tailored that suit for you," Mrs. Paxton cried. "And your derby! That was a gift from me."

Mrs. Paxton hung the "CLOSED" sign in the window and rustled back to Doc, who found the scent of her hair to be most reviving. With his waterlogged arm in her delicate hand, she led him into the shop, where men's finery hung all around on the walls and shelves. The thought of dressing again in dry clothes was almost as appealing as Mrs. Paxton's blue eyes.

"And how is business of late?" Doc said.

"Better," she replied. "Stay here a moment, I have to dismiss the tailor and the ironing woman."

The other merchants on Randolph Street had raised their eyebrows when the thirtyish, lovely, blond widow decided to manage the store herself, after her husband passed away. Doc had been a little leery himself, but to his surprise and finally to his delight, the shop had fared well under Mrs. Paxton. It had taken nearly five years of subsequent visits for their respect and friendship to blossom into something more. Doc had been the slow one, said Mrs. Paxton. Now he was thankful that he had an educated, handsome woman to spend time with, especially after a rough case.

"Look at you," she said as she emerged from the rear of the shop. "Were you caught in a flash flood?"

"Do forgive me for being out of sorts," Doc replied with his lifeless hat in hand. "As you know, my business is often of an indelicate nature. Would you mind if I sat down?"

"Ever the gentleman," she replied. "Even when you're wet and half dead."

He took her chin in his fingers.

"'A face, with nature's own hand painted, hast thou,'" Doc said.

"I love Shakespeare," she replied.

Mrs. Paxton was gazing at him with a familiar fire in her blue eyes. Doc could never be sure that look would be there each time he returned to her. She was always a mystery to him, even when they shared things beyond friendship. Never had she pressed him to stay or to marry her. And he thought she preferred their arrangement to wedlock, even though he expected to come back one day to find her married to a prominent San Franciscan.

"May I undress you?" she asked in a whisper.

"I was hoping for it," he replied.

"Why didn't you ask me?"

"I thought it rude just to blurt it out," he replied.

She kissed him for a long time before her hands went to work on his buttons. Off came the soggy coat and vest. The wet silk shirt was pronounced ruined before it hit the floor with a dull plop. Her lips and fingers traced the lines of his chest and stomach, stirring unkindled energies inside Doc. Before she reached the buckle of his belt, however, Mrs. Paxton rose up with a sharp cry.

"What's that?" she cried.

She was pointing toward the .38 Diamondback lodged in Doc's belt. He had forgotten to stash the weapon in his toolbox. His wagon and his mule were stabled a few doors down. He had not been thinking when he brought the gun into Mrs. Paxton's shop.

"Forgive me," he said. "The roads are so bad in Oregon that I was under advisement not to take my wagon. If you'll excuse me . . ."

"No, don't go," she said. "It's all right."

Mrs. Paxton's blue eyes were frozen on the revolver. She was not scared, but rather enthralled by the surprise of

Doc's weapon. Her delicate hand was at the lace throat of her collar. She seemed to be contemplating the work of her infrequent lover for the first time.

"You've never brought that here before," she said.

"Rest assured that I do not enjoy carrying it," Doc replied.

"Did you have to kill anyone?" she whispered.

"No, fortunately not," he replied. "Although my miscreant partner was insistent upon a cloudburst of rifle slugs. If he hadn't saved my life..."

"You were almost killed?" she cried.

"I regret saying that," Doc replied, taking the Diamondback from his belt.

"May I hold it?" asked Mrs. Paxton.

"I'd rather you didn't."

"Please."

Doc was amused by Mrs. Paxton's expression as she hoisted the weight of the pistol. She held it at eye level and made noises that she believed to be gunshots. No doubt, thought Doc, she had been reading adventure magazines again. The passionate moment was rapidly slipping away, forcing Doc to remember his manners.

"Mrs. Paxton," he said. "If I may take my leave of you, I wish to find a hotel with a hot bath."

"I won't hear of it, Mr. Weatherbee," she replied. "Why, I have a tub in the back. And it just happens to be full of hot water."

"My pistol," Doc said....

As he settled into the steaming tub, Mrs. Paxton cracked the door and called to him through the opening.

"You've come at the right time," she said. "The opera is in town. It's a tour from Europe."

"What are they singing?" Doc replied.

"*Die Fledermaus,*" said Mrs. Paxton. "I hear the production is wonderful."

"Ah, yes. *The Bat,*" Doc said. "An odd name for an operetta. Leave it to the Austrians for whimsical titles. I do so enjoy Johann Strauss, however."

"Of course, I'll have to outfit you again," she said. "I have some fine silks in from the Orient. I had to wait a month for them."

"If you don't mind, I'll have another long suit just like the one I was wearing," he replied. "And another derby."

"You certainly know what you prefer," she said.

Yes, Doc thought, torching the end of his cheroot: an operetta, a fine meal, and a merry widow. What more could he ask after a hard mission? If only he could find a way to avoid Raider for the rest of the week.

Raider avoided the telegraph office when he found his way to Telegraph Hill. He knew there would be a remittance—pay and expenses—from Allan Pinkerton. But there might also be another assignment, and Raider wasn't ready to take to the field again. Let Doc handle the paper part of it, Raider thought. He was heading for the edge of Chinatown, where Reva Summers kept her bordello. Raider wondered if she would still be mad at him.

He stopped in front of the whitewashed house, gazing up at the second-story window of her room. His worldly possessions—saddle, bedroll, rifle, and canteen—hung at his right shoulder. He went up the wooden steps and let himself in the front door. The parlor, all red and flowery, was empty. As he turned toward the staircase, he heard a familiar voice.

"Damn your black eyes, Raider," said Reva Summers. "Get your muddy boots off my Persian rug!"

Reva came down the stairs with her bosom, perfumed and powdered, blushing as red as her painted mouth. She was mad, bitch mad, with a pink glow that showed through her flimsy peignoir. The last time Raider had seen her, she was chasing him down the street with a butcher knife in her hand. She had been "a might frazzled," or so Raider had to explain to the constable who broke up the fight. Women could sure as hell hold a grudge, he thought.

"What makes you think you can shove in here like this?" Reva cried at the bottom of the stairs. "Who the hell do you think you are, Mr. Pinkerton?"

"Aw, put a noose around it," Raider replied. "I've been in the saddle for two days, and I'm draggin'. Either throw me out or show me where I can stow my gear."

The last time, he had found his gear on the front porch with a note that said, "Git out and don't never come back." Raider wondered if she would let him stay this time. She was capable of staying mad for weeks and weeks.

"Have you forgotten—"

"I ain't forgot nothin'," Raider replied. "But I'm tired and I hurt, Reva. I sure as hell don't need none of your buffalo biscuits. I'm sorry about the last time. If you didn't want me trying one of the new girls, you should have said something. I paid her, fair and square. But I don't give a pig's ass about your Persian rug or your butcher knife. All I want is a bath, a decent meal, and some sleep."

They were locked up, eye to eye. Reva teetered, her ruby lower lip extended in a pout that weakened Raider's anger and his knees. When she moved, her generous proportions shifted under her nightwear. She had just climbed out of bed, having slept away most of the day. After all, he thought, she did her work at night.

"What'll it be?" Raider demanded.

"Oh, it didn't bother me that you tried one of the other girls," she replied. "You should have asked me, though."

"Don't be so holy," Raider said. "Righteous don't fit on you."

"I can't be righteous until you make an honest woman out of me," she replied.

"We ain't got that much time," he said.

"Damn your black eyes," she cried. "Get out of here!"

"Have it your way," Raider replied. "I'll see if Belle will take me in."

Raider wheeled around on his heels, clomping toward the door with his muddy boots, hoping she would come after him. He did not want to go to Belle's. Belle was skinny, and her house wasn't nearly as good as Reva's place. A hurricane-lamp globe smashed against the door next to Raider's head. It hurt him to open the door and start down the front steps. He wanted to stay. Slippers treaded softly behind him.

"Raider. Raider, damn it. Don't leave, Raider."

He stopped on the stoop with his back to her. Her soft hand encircled his forearm. When he turned toward her, she shook her thick head of black hair and kissed his mouth. The saddle and the bedroll fell from Raider's shoulders. She melted into him.

"We really mix it up, don't we?" Reva whispered. "Oh, Raider, I've been so lonely for you."

"How can you be lonely in your line of work?" Raider said.

"Don't pick at it," Reva replied. "Let it be for now, Raider."

"Sometimes it sticks in my gizzard," Raider said.

"You know I'll quit tupping if you marry me," she said.

"Yeah, I know," he replied.

But he could never ask her to stop, no more than she could expect him to settle down. They were something of a pair, he thought. Both in demand from their clients, both expected to make everything all right. A couple of real mercenaries.

"Wo Hop," Reva shouted back into the house. "Wo Hop, get out here now."

An elderly Chinese man appeared through the threshold. He smiled when he saw Raider. All of Reva's employees liked to see Raider in the house. Reva was much calmer when Raider was in residence.

"Do something with Raider's saddle," Reva said. "I'll take care of his saddle horn," she whispered sidelong to Raider.

"I shine," Wo Hop said. "Good shine, Mr. Raider. Boots too. You want give me rifle and pistol?"

"They stay with me," Raider replied.

"Must we?" Reva said.

"Can't be too careful," Raider said. "There's a few men around that wouldn't mind splattering me all over Chinatown."

"You're so dangerous," she whispered. "Let's go back into the house before the Citizens Committee attacks us."

Raider figured she would drag him into the bathhouse. Reva didn't allow dirty men to sleep with her girls. Raider unbuckled his gunbelt and started for the hall that led to the back rooms of the house. Reva stopped him.

"No, not the bathhouse," she said. "I want you in my own tub. It's new. Italian marble. Cost me a hundred in gold."

"I ain't drew my pay yet," Raider said. "I'm flatter than a snake's pecker."

"You'll think of some way to pay me," she said. "In my tub, it'll be more exciting."

In her own dressing room, she stood back and watched as Raider stripped. His powerful body was pale from the cold, wet, sunless weather of Oregon. Reva knew every scar that lined his legs, arms, and torso. He caught her staring at him with her green eyes.

"What are you gawking at?" he said.

She was looking below his stomach.

"I always remember how big you are, but I don't really believe it until I see you again," she said. "You're a fine cut of man, Raider. Get into that tub."

The water she poured over him was perfumed and oily, but it was hot and it relieved some of his sore spots. He couldn't remember the last time his body was free of pain. When he was covered with water, Reva moved around behind him and started to rub his shoulders with a soapy washcloth.

"Ow! Ease off, darling," Raider said.

She saw the closed gash on his shoulder. Doc had cauterized the wound to stop the bleeding. It still ached like hell.

"Gunshot?" Reva asked.

"I caught a low-hanging branch," Raider replied. "Oregon is thick with trees."

"You poor wretch," she said.

"I'll wretch you!"

He tried to yank her into the tub, but she pulled away.

"Not yet," she replied. "You know the house rules. I want to make sure you're clean. All of you."

Reva knelt at the side of the tub, working on Raider with her silky fingers, lathering his chest and stomach. She didn't resist when Raider pushed her hands below the surface of the water. As he became more excited, her hands rose above the surface. When she tried to leave for a moment to wash his legs, he pulled her back. His eyes were half closed, and he lay back against the marble tub, his rugged jaw slack and his mouth open.

"I want it," he said.

"Not yet," she replied. "Not just yet."

"When? I'm plumb tuckered out."

"We'll see."

Reva made him stand and then poured more buckets of hot water over his body. She dabbed him with a towel, lingering on the areas that required extraordinary attention. Raider wasn't sure how much longer he could keep his hands off her. The tease was unbearable.

"Into the bed," she said when Raider was dry.

"Let me get my rifle and my forty-four," Raider replied.

"Do you always have to—"

"I sleep better," he said.

He followed her into her white room, putting the rifle under the bed and the .44 in the drawer of her nightstand.

"Feel better?" she asked.

"Not as good as I'm gonna feel," he replied.

He pulled her close to him for the first time. Her nipples brushed the hair of his chest, evoking a sigh from her thick lips. As he kissed her, she hoisted up her nightgown, rubbing herself against his protruding manhood. They tumbled onto her downy bed. Raider was on top of her, working his hips between her thighs, trying to enter her with a quick thrust, the way she liked it. But Reva stopped him short of penetration.

"What's wrong now?" he asked, thinking that those were the three words he used most with women.

"Wrong time," she said. "I'm bleeding."

"Oh, hell," Raider replied. "I ain't afraid to wade in the red river."

"Let's do it the other way."

Raider rolled over and looked up at the ceiling.

"You're the only one ever done that to me," Raider lied.

"I learned it from a French girl who used to work for me," Reva replied. "I want you in my mouth, Raider."

"Somehow it don't seem natural."

"You want me to stop?" she asked.

But she knew he didn't want her to stop. She laughed and ran her hands over his chest, kissing his nipples, working her way down to the knotty lines of his belly. She kissed the scar where an Apache flint knife had almost disemboweled him. He groaned a little.

"I'll make you forget the pain," she said. "Oh, how I'll make you forget!"

Her head hovered for a moment before falling the entire length of his masculinity. Raider shivered, almost unable to control the pleasure that swept over him. He couldn't fight it. Reva was sure as hell making him forget about Oregon.

"Don't stop," Raider moaned. "Damn it all, Reva, you sure know how to get to me. That's finer than frog hair."

And she didn't stop until she had evidence of his pleasure.

After a thick steak and a pound of fried potatoes, Raider fell asleep on Reva's goose-down mattress. His slumber was deep and dreamless, and when he awoke in the late evening he suffered the disorientation of waking in an unfamiliar place. Lying still in the bed, he allowed his eyes to adjust in the darkness. The tinny, jingle-jangle music of the piano rose up from downstairs, counterpointed by the buzzy clatter of male and female voices. It was Saturday night, so the bordello was jumping with girls and their clients in every room. Raider tendered thoughts of finding the Creole girl he had enjoyed on his visit before, but he quickly remembered Reva's temper—and her butcher knife.

Where the hell was Reva anyway? Probably downstairs,

he thought, directing the men to their various pleasures. Her perfume lingered in the air around Raider, filling his senses, rekindling the same fires that Reva had doused earlier. Damn her and her strange tastes, Raider thought. He wanted something along ordinary lines, something where he was on top.

Before he could call for her, Reva slipped in through the door. She tiptoed up next to the bed and gazed down at Raider, who feigned sleep. Her soft fingers touched the coarse, black hair that fell over Raider's forehead. Raider startled her when he grabbed her wrist and pulled her down next to him.

"You scab," she cried. "Pretending to be asleep."

"I'm not sleepy now," Raider replied. "I'm wanting to love on you some, magnolia."

"You don't love anyone but yourself," she said, fighting his efforts to subdue her.

"I love it when you fight me."

But Reva did not resist for long. Raider pulled her down, finding her lips with his mouth, trapping her in his arms, turning her mock-anger into passion. She began to work her hips, grinding her pelvis against his midsection. Her tongue rolled outside her mouth, licking his mustache.

"I can stay on top," she whispered.

"No you can't," Raider replied. "I want it my way."

They wrestled around until Raider was on top. Her thighs parted, and his hips fell into place. Reva kneaded the sinewy muscles of his shoulders as he prodded her, trying to enter. Raider gazed down at her lovely face, anticipating desires that would never be consummated. Suddenly she tensed beneath him, denying his feverish attempt to penetrate her.

"What?" he asked.

"Shh, listen," she replied.

"I don't hear nothing," Raider said.

"There it is again," she insisted.

"Aw, punkin, it ain't nothing."

But Raider finally heard it too. A commotion, loud voices, and sounds of breakage rattled through the house. The piano stopped. Another crashing sound. A man's voice was shouting above the others. Then a woman screamed.

"Son of a bitch," Raider groaned.

He was losing his excitement.

"Honey," Reva said. "Please, go see what it is."

"Aw, don't you have one of your boys here tonight?" Raider said. "I mean, damn it all, Reva."

"Please, Raider," she replied. "You're used to..."

Why was it so hard to resist the sweet tones of her voice?

"Aw, cuss it all!"

He came steaming out of bed, stepped into his trousers, and took his .44 from the drawer in her nightstand. Whatever the trouble, Raider was going to end it quickly, so he could get back into bed with Reva. The upstairs hall was crowded with girls and men who parted abruptly when Raider's half-naked frame strode through them. He waved the pistol, making quite a spectacle as he hustled toward the room at the end of the hall where the disturbance was taking place.

"Aw right," Raider barked to the spectators, "all of you citizens get back in your rooms before I have to shoot you."

Doors slammed quickly at the commanding tone of his voice. Raider stood in front of the doorway at the end of the hall, which was also closed. He tried the knob, but it was locked. Silence inside the room. With one kick from his foot, the door sprang open. Raider stepped in, expecting to see a distraught client with an unwilling chippy. He got a lot more than he bargained for.

"What the hell?"

On the floor lay a half-dressed, dark-skinned woman. Over her stood a young blond man, about Raider's height, but skinnier and eight or ten years his junior. A kid, Raider thought. The kid held a buffalo rifle in his hands. The octagonal barrel of a .50 caliber Sharps was pointed at the woman's head. The hammer was pulled back, ready to fire.

"Make one move and this bitch is dead," the kid said.

"Now, just hold on, boy," Raider replied. "Don't do nothing too stupid, leastways till we can talk a spell."

The woman was frozen, unable to move or speak.

"That Sharps is an awful lot of gun for shooting one whore," Raider said. "Drop it, son. You don't want—"

"I ain't your son and I ain't dropping it," the kid said. "This whore knows something, and I aim to get it out of her."

Raider considered dropping him right there. But there was a hesitancy in the kid's voice that stopped him. The kid might be short-fused and headstrong—like Raider when he was a kid—but he was scared, too. And the Sharps would turn the woman's head into chopped meat if Raider shot the kid and the kid squeezed off a round before he fell.

"Looks like we got ourselves a standoff," Raider said.

"No standoff," the kid cried. "You're gonna let me out of here, and I'm taking this bitch with me."

"I can't," Raider said. "See, I know your rifle, boy. You got a rolling breech there. One shot. You might kill her, but I'd plug you before you moved an inch."

Raider watched the kid as he contemplated the circumstances. He was dressed in buckskins, like he had just ridden in off the range. Floppy felt hat. He sure as hell wasn't from Frisco, not with those soft-tanned Indian boots.

"You mean you don't care if I shoot her?" the kid asked.

"What's that whore to me?" Raider bluffed. "There's plenty more where she came from."

"No!" the woman cried. "You pig. You bastard."

"I ain't afraid to shoot her," the kid replied.

"You got to ask yourself a question, boy," Raider said. "You can have two dead people or none. What'll it be?"

The kid's blue eyes were glazed.

"You ever kill anyone before?" Raider asked.

Raider could tell from the kid's sick expression that he had never sent anyone to their reward. Raider had to press. He had to make him give it up.

"Look, son," Raider continued. "You say this woman knows something that you need. But if you kill her, you don't get it. And if I kill you, then everything's pretty much shot, ain't it?"

"You're going to let me out of here," the kid replied. "And I'm taking this Sioux squaw with me."

The woman was an Indian. Looking at her, Raider had thought she was Mexican. The kid was full of surprises.

"I can't allow you to leave," Raider said, thumbing back the hammer of the .44. "So drop it, now."

"If I put down my rifle, you'll tell the law."

Sweat beads were pouring off the kid's forehead.

"I won't tell anyone," Raider said. "You let her go and I'll talk to you."

"How do I know your word is true?" the kid asked.

"I'm a Pinkerton," Raider replied. "I'd never lie to you without a good reason."

"I can't," the kid said.

"I'm going to kill you in five seconds if you don't."

Raider pointed the .44 at the kid's head, forcing him to look down the barrel. The kid dropped the rifle and sat down on the bed. The woman fainted. Raider took the Sharps and unloaded the thick brass cartridge.

"Okay, Reva," Raider called into the hallway.

She rushed up to the threshold.

"Should I send someone for the constable?" Reva asked.

"You want the law around here?" Raider asked.

"Hell no," she replied. "What are we going to do with him?"

"I promised I'd talk to him," Raider said. "So he's going to tell me why he wanted this woman."

"Then what?" Reva asked.

"Then we go back to bed," Raider replied.

He turned back to the kid, who was staring down at the woman on the floor.

"Now, boy, suppose you tell me why you had this cannon pointed at her head," Raider said.

"She knows," the kid replied. "I'm telling you, she knows."

He told Raider the story. Raider listened, at first with a sense of curiosity, and then with resolve. And when the kid had finished, Raider did not go back to bed with Reva. Instead, he went to find Doc.

CHAPTER TWO

With the music of Strauss still buzzing in his ears, Doc shifted in a half-slumber, feeling the warmth of the full-figured woman next to him. He pulled her close until her bare shoulder touched his lips for a moment. Slowly he began to nibble on her, working his way up her neck toward her mouth. When Mrs. Paxton felt him, she stirred also, returning his kisses with an uninhibited tongue, half caught in the trance herself. They were rising toward something more when the banging reached their ears. It had been the sound that awakened Doc in the first place.

For a moment, they both pretended they didn't hear it. But the rapping came back again, rude and intrusive. They opened their eyes and listened in the darkness. Doc did not want to get out of bed on a cold San Francisco night. Then, suddenly, the truth occurred to him. He let out an exasperated breath.

"That pounding is all too familiar," he muttered.

"It's just a tramp," Mrs. Paxton replied. "Or maybe a husband, trying to get a new pair of pants to change into before he incriminates himself with his wife."

"Doubtful," Doc replied. "I'd recognize the cadence of those fists in the middle of an earthquake."

"I'll go," said Mrs. Paxton.

"I'll see to it," Doc replied. "Although I wonder how he found me here? I've never told him about you."

"Him?" she called.

But Doc had risen and was stepping into a freshly pressed pair of woolen trousers chosen for him by Mrs. Paxton. He left her and hurried into the shop, wondering if he could be wrong about the identity of the intruder's knocking. But he wasn't wrong. When Doc turned up the gas lamp, he saw Raider standing at the door, peering in through the etched glass. When Doc threw open the door, Raider was startled by the hatred in his partner's face. Doc was usually more composed.

"Sorry, Doc..."

"This is an unpleasant surprise, Raider," Doc barked. "You've broken your promise to me. It hasn't been forty-eight hours since I last laid eyes on you."

"Doc, will you just listen?"

"What the devil, man?"

"Doc, there's this kid..."

"Are you insane?"

"He's in trouble, Doc."

"So are you!"

"Don't be that way, Doc."

"Are you simply drunk or have you been smoking opium?"

"Doc," said Mrs. Paxton. "Is everything all right?"

Raider removed his Stetson when he saw Mrs. Paxton in her white dressing gown. His mustache hid the churlish grin that spread over his mouth. He could tell that Doc was "a might riled," but he couldn't help having a little fun with the circumstances.

"Pardon me, ma'am," Raider said bashfully.

"I'm Mrs. Paxton," she replied.

"*Mrs*. Paxton!" Raider chuckled.

"I'm a widow," she said.

"I don't mean to buffalo in like this, Mrs. Paxton," Raider said. "I'm what you might call Doc's—"

"Associate," Doc said without humor. "Soon to be former or perhaps deceased associate."

"This is sort of important, Mrs. Paxton," Raider continued, ignoring Doc to plead to his companion.

"Can't this wait until daylight?" Doc asked.

"Not if we can help it," Raider replied. "But if it's all the same to you, my evening has been shot all to hell too. And I think you should hear it now, while it's still fresh in everyone's mind, Doc."

Mrs. Paxton had stepped forward and was listening to them. Doc saw her from the corner of his eye. Her face was flushed and her eyes were gleaming. She had sported the same expression when he had shown her his Diamondback pistol. She was drawn in by anything mysterious or dangerous. Daring, thought Doc, was a feminine virtue.

"Are you the one who saved Mr. Weatherbee's life?" Mrs. Paxton asked Raider.

"I humbly take the blame for that," Raider said.

"I'd love to hear all about it," she replied. "Doc never tells me—"

"That's enough, Raider," Doc said.

"So, you coming along?" Raider asked.

Doc glanced at Mrs. Paxton.

"It's perfectly fine with me," she said. "Go with your partner, Doc. I don't mind. In fact, I'll come along with you if you need me."

"You don't have to do that," Raider said. "I mean, well, we ain't going to a fancy part of town or nothing like that."

"I can imagine," Doc grumbled.

"Now, Doc," said Mrs. Paxton. "This gentleman did save your life."

"No more times than he's put my life in jeopardy," Doc replied. "This is just an example of his recklessness. Waking me up in the middle of the night."

"It'll only take an hour of your time," Raider said.

"How the devil did you find me, anyway?" Doc asked.

"Cost me a dollar to get it out of the stable boy," Raider replied.

"Thank you for reminding me," Doc said. "I must look in on Judith immediately."

"Judith!" cried Mrs. Paxton.

"His mule," Raider replied. "And believe me, Mrs. Paxton, you're a lot prettier than—"

"We'll take the wagon to wherever we're going," Doc said.

"Then you'll come along?" Raider asked.

"Is there any other way to be rid of you, Raider?"

As they rolled through the quiet, muddy streets of San Francisco, Raider bounced on the seat of the Studebaker wagon, which was drawn by the gristly haunches of Doc's mule, Judith. Raider had never understood Doc's attachment and affection for the ragged critter. To Raider, one horse was pretty much the same as another. It seemed odd for a city-bred man, a man with a Harvard education, to take so to a mule, one of God's less intelligent creatures. But then, once in a while Doc surprised him—like the widow lady.

"How come you never mentioned Mrs. Paxton?" Raider asked.

"Somehow, I didn't think you'd take the matter to heart," Doc said. "She's a fine lady, and I won't have her disparaged."

"She's quite a looker," Raider said. "I wouldn't mind—"

"Where are we going?" Doc asked.

"Sutter Street," Raider replied. "Turn here."

Doc tugged at the reins and Judith pulled right, heading up another steady incline.

"She certainly needs the exercise," Doc said.

"The widow?" Raider said. "Or the mule?"

"I've heard quite enough out of you!" Doc said. "If you don't stop, I'll be forced to shoot you."

Raider laughed, but he quickly dropped the subject. Doc needed to be fresh and clear-thinking when they got back to Reva's place, and Raider's ribbing would not help matters any. He wondered how Doc would react to the kid's incredible story. Doc might not see things the same way.

"I see we're sinking into degeneracy," Doc said as the wagon rolled down the hill and up another. "I had no idea that your friends were so elite, Raider."

"If I can't say nothin' about your widow-woman, then

you can't say nothing about my lady friends," Raider replied.

"Would that be one of your friends up ahead?" Doc asked.

As they approached Sutter Street, Reva Summers ran toward them, her silky peignoir fluttering in the night breezes. Raider bounded down off the wagon and ran to meet her, putting his hands on her white shoulders.

"What happened?" Raider asked.

"The kid," she replied as she caught her breath. "The kid got out."

"But I had him locked in that room," Raider said.

"He kicked the door down," she replied. "It took him twenty minutes after you left, but he did it. He's gone wild."

"Where did he go? Which direction?"

"He took that girl, the one he was after, and dragged her into the alley," Reva replied.

"How long ago?" Raider asked.

"Just now!" she replied. "Just a minute ago."

"Your kid has slipped under the fence," Doc rejoined.

"Yeah, but he can't get far dragging that woman with him," Raider replied. "I'll follow him down the alley, Doc. You go down to the bottom of the hill and ride back and forth on the cross street. I think it's Carson Street."

"That's it," Reva said.

"Raider," Doc said. "This is no affair of mine. Why don't I just—"

"Do it," Raider said. "Then we'll be square for Oregon."

"All right," Doc replied. "But the devil take you if I hear about your saving my life again!"

Doc turned Judith down the hill and started for Carson Street.

"He's wearing buckskins," Raider called.

"I doubt if we'll find him," Doc cried.

"It'll be just like flushing a Fulton County whitetail," Raider shouted back. "Hurry, Doc."

Raider ran back up the hill and through the house, causing another ruckus as he shot down the steps into the back alley. He looked quickly to his right and left, wondering which way a frightened, crazy kid would run. If he was dragging the Sioux woman, he wouldn't go uphill. And she certainly wasn't going to make it easy for the kid to run away.

Raider started slowly down the dark alley, listening in the cool, city dampness for sounds of breathing and scuffling between the houses. A short, muffled shriek rose momentarily on the night air and then was gone. Raider marked it and continued down the alley, taking his first opportunity to turn toward the direction of the sound. He stopped between two houses to listen again.

Nothing. Had the kid heard him coming? Raider pulled his .44 out of his holster, continuing on to the next street, which was better lighted than the alley. Raider stole along the street, heading downhill, looking between the houses for the kid and the woman. A crash in a doorway gave the kid away. Raider ducked low, watching the shadows. Before he moved again, the kid came out onto the street, holding the woman by the hair. His knife blade was pressed to the dark skin of her throat.

"Don't be dumb, kid," Raider shouted. "I want to help you."

"I'll cut her if you come after me," the kid cried.

Raider sat still, listening for the thud of Judith's hooves and the rattling of her harness. Where the hell was Doc? Finally he heard the wagon on Carson Street at the end of the incline, where the street formed a natural valley.

"All right," Raider shouted. "Run on out of here. Just git gone and don't cause us no more trouble."

With that, the kid released the blade and grabbed the Sioux woman's wrist, pulling her toward a rendezvous with Doc. When the kid ran out in front of the wagon, Doc almost came up out of his seat. The kid wheeled to avoid a collision. He saw Doc, but didn't make the connection until Doc pulled out the Diamondback and aimed it at his head.

"That's a fine place to stop," Doc said. "Let go of the woman."

The Sioux woman tore away from the kid's grasp, leaving him alone in the street. The kid broke into a run, but Doc quickly applied the whip to Judith's hindquarters, causing her to bolt forward. Raider emerged on the street just in time to see Doc leap from the wagon to tackle the kid, driving him into the muddy roadway.

Doc jumped to his feet, and the kid was on him immediately, swinging furiously. Raider just stood there, watching them go at it. The kid's knife was lost in the mud, so it would be an even fight. Doc took a fist on the forehead but promptly jumped back, measuring the power and angle of the kid's blows. The attack was strong and savage, but the kid's awkwardness left him vulnerable to Doc's left hand.

Doc flicked several quick shots to the kid's temple, stunning him slightly with each successive blow. But the kid kept after him, swinging wildly. Doc was holding his own, certainly not taking a beating; but the kid wasn't going down. Raider thought it best to intercede.

"Let me try it," Raider said, stepping between the kid and Doc. "Come and get it, boy."

Raider used his forearm to block the kid's next shot, answering the deflected blow with a crushing right to the lad's chin. The kid buckled, but he didn't fall. He staggered backward, reeling and still throwing punches into the wind. Raider rared back to hit him between the eyes, but the kid went down to his knees.

"Don't hit him again," Doc said. "You might hurt your hand."

The kid flopped into the remains of a mud puddle.

"He's tough for a beanpole," Raider said. "I caught him square on the jawbone and he took it."

"What are we going to do with him?" Doc asked.

But before Raider could speculate, the angry Sioux woman was on top of the kid, beating him with tiny, clenched fists. Raider pulled her off, pinning her arms behind her as she cursed the man on the ground. Doc started to help the beaten kid to his feet.

"It seems that you keep quite pleasant company in your off hours, Raider," Doc said with a half-smile. "I must admit that you've finally drawn me into this thing."

"Having a good time, Doc?" Raider said sarcastically.

"Suffice it to say that my curiosity had been piqued."

"What?"

"I'm interested," Doc replied. "I'm simply interested."

Raider tipped back his Stetson and studied the kid, who slouched in Reva's cane-backed rocking chair, staring down at the red and blue Persian rug. Reva had forced the kid out of the smelly buckskins and into her marble tub. Wo Hop had rustled up a pair of boots, a pair of denim trousers, and a gray woolen shirt. The kid didn't stink anymore, Raider thought, and in the different clothes, he didn't look so wild and uncivilized. A dark spot had raised itself on his chin, where Raider had popped him. The Indian girl had clawed him a little on the right side of his face too. The damned kid sure looked beaten, Raider thought.

"Maybe you should tell Doc now," Raider said quietly.

Nothing from the kid.

"Let him take his own time," Doc said. "He might not want to talk right away. He's probably weary from all of his histrionics."

The kid looked up at Doc for the first time and then glanced over in Raider's direction.

"He means you raised some hell, boy," Raider said, qualifying Doc's high-toned language. "And you're tired because of it."

The kid looked back down at the rug, not saying anything.

"The cat's got his tongue," said Reva Summers.

She was standing behind Doc, clad in a black, feather-necked dressing robe. The ladies always went formal for Doc, Raider thought. As soon as Doc had kissed the back of Reva's hand, Reva had changed her robe and begun to act all ladylike. Raider tried not to let it grate on him; he should have been used to Doc's charm, but it still ticked him when Doc gave a sweeping bow, his pearl-gray derby in his gentlemanly hand.

"Miss Summers," Doc said to Reva.

"Yes, Mr. Weatherbee?" she replied eagerly.

"I was wondering if you might see fit to provide us with a pot of fresh tea," Doc said. "I think we may be waiting awhile for this young gentleman to speak."

"I'll see to it at once," Reva replied.

"I'm most appreciative," Doc said.

"I ain't drinking tea," Raider chimed in. "Bring me a pot of black coffee."

"You'll drink what the rest of us drink," Reva snapped.

"Look at that, Doc," Raider quipped. "You done turned her into a lady."

"You could stand to be a little more mannerly yourself," Reva shot back. "Like your partner here!"

"I figured that was coming," Raider muttered.

Reva turned up her nose a bit and stormed out.

"Splendid girl," Doc said, half smiling.

"I'll trade her for one night with the widow," Raider snapped.

"Enough," Doc said, turning his attention back to the kid. "I simply wanted Miss Summers out of the room when our friend here begins to talk."

"I ain't your friend," the kid muttered.

"That's a start," Doc said. "And even if we aren't going to be friends, you might at least tell me your name."

"Told me his name was Johnny," Raider said.

"Do you have a last name, Johnny?" Doc asked.

For the second time, the kid looked up at Doc. Doc was momentarily disarmed by the vivid white rings in the kid's blue eyes. Wolfish irises, like the timber wolves they had seen in Oregon. Doc regarded him closely: strong, narrow nose; long hair that had become lighter after Reva's shampoo; an outdoor complexion worn by sun and wind, but still youthful. The kid's expression was drawn and angry, but Doc somehow could not think of him as an adversary.

"Raider tells me that you're in some sort of trouble," Doc said, lighting his cheroot.

"I told the Texan everything," the kid said.

"I'm from Arkansas, not Texas," Raider replied.

"We'll haggle over geography another time," Doc said. "But right now I want an explanation. Otherwise, I call the local constable and you will spend the night in jail for disturbing the peace."

"No!" the kid cried. "No law! I don't want the law!"

"Then you'll begin by telling me your last name," Doc insisted.

The kid thought about it for a moment.

"I guess it can't make things any worse," the kid replied. "Welton. My name is Johnny Welton."

"Welton?" Raider said. "Are you any kin to Jack Welton?"

"You knew him?" the kid asked.

"I used to hunt with him, about ten years back," Raider said. "Didn't he have a lodge in Wyoming?"

"That must have been the year he followed the elk herd down south," Johnny said. "He wouldn't let me go on that trip."

"You are kin to him then," Raider said.

"He was my pa," the kid drawled.

"Was? You mean he's dead?" Doc asked.

"Johnny claims his pa was murdered," Raider said.

"You have proof of that?" Doc inquired.

"Little Bright Wing," Johnny replied.

"I beg your pardon?" Doc said.

"That's the Sioux chippy I came after," Johnny said. "I think she knows who killed my father."

Doc tapped his ash into a spittoon. Then he leaned back and drew on the cheroot, billowing up clouds of smoke over his head. Raider coughed a little, but Doc didn't hear him.

"It seems this is more complex than I had imagined," Doc said. "You'd better tell me everything, Johnny. The same way you told it to Raider."

Johnny sat forward in the rocking chair, glancing back and forth between Doc and Raider. He was trying to trust them, Raider thought. He probably hadn't told Raider everything at first. He sure as hell hadn't mentioned that his father was Jack Welton, the famous hunter. Johnny was opening his mouth to say something just as Reva entered with the pot of tea Doc had requested.

"Did I miss anything?" Reva asked.

"Johnny here told us the real name of your Mexican girl," Raider replied.

"You mean Maria?" Reva asked.

"Her true name seems to be Little Bright Wing," Doc rejoined. "And she's a full-blooded Sioux Indian, as far as we know."

"She told me she had just come up from the Baja," Reva said.

"Would you have taken her in if you'd known she was an Indian?" Doc asked.

"Sure," Reva replied. "Men pay plenty for exotic girls. I could have gotten another five bucks."

Doc stood up, politely taking Reva's hand and looking into her eyes with his most sincere countenance. It made Raider sick when Doc trotted out the suave demeanor. Still, Raider had to hand it to him—he could even transform Reva into a lady.

"Miss Summers," Doc said. "I was wondering if you would aid us in this investigation?"

"Doc, she can't—"

"Please, Raider," Reva said. "Doc was just about to say something to me."

"Yes, Reva," he continued. "I wish you would talk to the Indian girl for me. She might give up some useful information to one of her own gender."

"I've heard it all," Raider muttered.

Reva hurried out of the room, gleefully devoting herself to Doc's assigned task.

"Did you have to do that?" Raider moaned.

"She'll be out of our way," Doc replied. "And women will sometimes confide in each other. She might even learn something to our advantage."

Doc turned back to Johnny Welton, who had grown sullen again.

"I want you to tell me everything," Doc said. "Make your story logical: beginning, middle, and end. Don't leave out even the slightest detail."

"Why?" Johnny snapped. "Why should I tell you?"

"Because we are Pinkerton operatives," Doc said. "And if some wrong has occurred, then you may employ us, at our usual fee, to seek out the perpetrator and see that he is dealt with accordingly."

"And if you don't talk, we call the law," Raider said.

"Agreed," Doc rejoined.

"No! No law!" Johnny cried.

"You have an aversion to the authority of the law," Doc said. "Are you wanted for something, perhaps?"

"No, I just don't trust the law," Johnny replied. "I'm from Montana Territory, mister. Ain't much law out there. It's rough country. Miners and cattlemen, now. Men still shoot each other back home."

"I assure you that men are still shooting one another all over the world," Doc replied. "I suggest that we concentrate on your dilemma, Johnny."

"Does he always talk like this?" Johnny asked Raider.

"You'll get used to it," Raider replied. "Tell him about the Bar W."

"Bar W?" Doc said.

"My pa's ranch," Johnny replied. "Leastways, it used to be. Thirty thousand acres in all. You ever hear of the Elk Lodge Valley?"

Neither of them had.

"It's east of Butte and southeast of Helena," Johnny said. "My pa started there forty years ago. Back then it wasn't nothing but buffalo grass and bitterroot. He had a lodge there, but he hunted all over. And there were still buffalo around, so Pa would hunt for a living."

"You get the Sharps from him?" Raider asked.

"He had a whole collection of buffalo rifles," Johnny said. "They're still there, but I can't get to them. Not with . . ." He paused.

"Go on," Doc urged.

"Hell fire," Johnny said dejectedly. "What's the use? Nobody's on my side."

"Try us," Raider said.

Johnny stared at them like he was seeing them for the

first time. They were an unlikely pair—the slack-jawed Arkansas roughrider and the polished eastern dandy. But they seemed to be interested in his story.

"Things changed for my pa after my mother came along," Johnny said. "Her family settled on the range to the west of the Elk Lodge Valley. The boundaries touched. Her family was Swedes. They left Minnesota because my grandfather had a dream. He wanted to bring cattle into the territory. He tried, too, but the gold rush was on, so nobody took him serious-like."

"He was unsuccessful?" Doc asked.

"The winters wiped him out, or at least that's what Pa said," Johnny replied. "Folks thought he was crazy. But my momma didn't."

"No?" Doc said.

"She wouldn't give up," Johnny said. "She married Pa on the condition that he would start a ranch. The Bar W, he called it. She kept her father's dream alive. She made Pa into a rancher."

"There's a lot to be said for the motivating force of a woman," Doc said.

"They can really make you respectable," Raider said. "And take all the fun out of life."

"They can also make you unreasonably happy," Doc rejoined.

"I don't know if my momma made Pa happy or not," Johnny said. "She died in childbirth with my sister."

"Is your sister still alive?" Doc asked.

"Yes," Johnny replied. "I'll get to that."

"Let him tell it his way, Doc."

"After my momma died, Pa went back to running the lodge again," Johnny said. "He tried to forget about cattle. Trying to run a ranch with the winters had cost him a lot of money. So he went on with the lodge, trying to raise my sister and me the best he could. He sent us off to school a couple of times, but we always ran away and came home."

Johnny sighed and leaned over with his head in his hands.

"I don't know," he said woefully. "Things weren't the same with Pa as he got older. He couldn't stop thinking about Momma. He wanted to try cattle again. One day a group of men in Helena invited all the range men into town for a meeting. Told Pa how a man with a big herd could drive the steers south to Colorado or Kansas and make himself a lot of money. Said Montana was perfect for grazing and ranchers could beat the winters if they would get their steers south before the end of October."

"Is there anything to that, Raider?" Doc asked.

"I reckon," Raider replied. "Been a lot of talk all over about cattle since the gold rush died out."

"Continue, Mr. Welton."

"Like I told you, the Bar W is perfect for raising cattle," Johnny said. "The Elk Lodge Valley has mountains on all sides. The smaller ranges. The Little Belts are on the north. A ridge comes down from the north to the plain. It hooks around to form a natural basin. Steers can't go beyond the east ridge. I don't know why we call it the east ridge, 'cause it marks the western boundary of the Bar W. There's a canyon about eighty miles east that keeps the herd back and forth, grazing between the canyon and the mountains."

"A natural corral," Doc said. "How do you get the cows in and out of valley?"

"Drive 'em up Salt Lake City and take 'em through the pass," Johnny replied.

"On the east ridge?" Raider asked.

"Yeah, it's the only entrance to our property from the south and west," Johnny replied. "Leastways it was my property till Velma Ivery took over."

"Who?"

"The woman who married my pa a year ago," Johnny replied.

"That was when the trouble started," Raider said.

"My pa needed money to start up another herd," Johnny continued. "He sold land north of us to a man from St. Louis. The land wasn't worth much. I don't know why he wanted it. Said he had to get away from the city for his health."

"People run from cities for other reasons, too," Raider said. "Like when they been up to no good."

"Who was this man to your stepmother? And which one of them bought the land from your father?"

"Please, don't call her that," Johnny said. "No, Pa didn't sell it to her. He sold it to her brother, Sherman Ivery. I didn't like him from the start. He wanted the Bar W. I could see the look in his eyes every time they came to call at the lodge. Him with his slick hair and fine silk shirts. I'm willing to stake my life that he put her up to it."

"Why do you say that?" Doc asked.

"She didn't seem willing at first," Johnny replied. "But all of sudden she started up, sparking Pa. Pa never was too strong with women, and he really missed my momma. So they got married. Right away Sherman Ivery was wanting to throw in with Pa. But Pa told him to stay on his own range. That made Ivery mad. He didn't want to fence in his range."

"What was your . . . the woman's reaction when you father wouldn't throw in with her brother?" Doc asked.

"She didn't seem to care," Johnny replied. "She was kinda happy about it."

"Could it be that she was glad to be free of her brother, and happy to be with your father?" Doc speculated.

"Tell him about the takeover," Raider said.

Johnny shifted in the rocker, leaning back sadly.

"When I got back from taking cattle to the mines, I didn't recognize the lodge," Johnny said. "There were men on the porch and horses everywhere. When I went inside, Ivery and his sister were sitting at a table with a bunch of legal papers in front of them. They told me my father had been killed by renegade Indians. They claimed to have a will that left everything to Velma Ivery. They said that Diana, my sister, could stay on, but I had to leave."

"You should have pulled on him with that Sharps," Raider said. "He'd have fiddled with another bow then."

"How could I?" Johnny replied. "He had forty hired men."

"Did you appeal to the legal authorities?" Doc asked.

"The law?" Johnny chortled. "Possession is the law where I come from, mister."

"But surely there's a territorial justice somewhere in Montana?" Doc said.

"Bullets," Johnny said. "Bullets are all the justice I need."

"A bizarre way to lose a legacy," Doc said.

"Sounds smelly to me," Raider said. "Like a stunked-up polecat that's been lying in the road for a week."

Doc leaned back for a moment, contemplating Johnny Welton's story. If the kid was telling the truth, there were some interesting questions that had not been answered. He looked at the young man, who seemed more composed. Confession had released part of his burden.

"Mr. Welton," Doc said. "I'm going to trust you tonight. I want you to stay in this room. Have one of the girls if you like. Eat something and get a good night's sleep. Tomorrow morning I want you to send a wire to Mr. Allan Pinkerton requesting our services on your behalf. Do you have any money?"

"I got two hundred bucks in gold, from selling the beef to the copper miners," he replied.

"Remit one hundred dollars as a retainer to Mr. Pinkerton," Doc said. "It will be Sunday, so I'll give you the address in Chicago, to make sure it reaches him. We'll leave Monday morning for Montana."

"What if there's another assignment waiting for us at the telegraph office?" Raider asked.

"There won't be," Doc replied. "We haven't even wired the office that we're back in San Francisco. When Pinkerton receives this lad's request, the retainer will be on file and we'll be on our way to Montana."

"Don't forget to pick up our pay," Raider said.

Johnny Welton was watching them, and for the first time he had a smile on his thin lips.

"You really can help me, can't you?" he said.

"Have some faith," Raider said.

"You have to trust us," Doc rejoined. "And, in turn, we'll trust you. Good night, Mr. Welton. We'll talk again tomorrow."

Doc and Rider shook hands with the kid and stepped out into the hall.

"You want to talk to the girl now?" Raider asked.

"Not yet," Doc replied. "I think we should discuss what we've heard, however."

Raider couldn't agree more.

CHAPTER THREE

In her special parlor, Reva poured tea for Doc and a cup of strong coffee for Raider. Doc lifted the cup to his lips, remarking about the blend of the Orange Pekoe, which delighted Reva to no end. Raider, resting in a plush chair, ignored Doc's cultured banter and just swigged from his steaming coffee cup. Reva rarely invited strangers into her private room; Doc had warranted a special invitation.

"Did the girl reveal anything pertinent?" Doc asked.

"Nothing," Reva replied. "She wouldn't even talk. I tell you, I'm not keeping her on after this."

"Reva," Raider said. "If you don't mind, Doc and I would like to be alone right now."

"Oh, just like that, eh!" Reva scowled.

"That's not necessary, Raider," Doc said. "Miss Summers, my inarticulate friend, in his own clumsy way, is trying to tell you that it's for your own good that you mustn't have knowledge of the matter we'll be discussing. We've taken on the case of the young man upstairs, and you would only be endangering yourself to know any details of our discourse."

"I understand perfectly," Reva said, casting a derisive glance at Raider as she tripped away.

"Does anything but honey ever come out of your mouth?" Raider said, shaking his head.

"Please, I'm trying to concentrate, Raider," Doc said. "And you should do the same."

"Don't think I ain't," Raider replied. "I already spotted something that don't fit."

"I'm listening," Doc said.

"It's the Indian thing," Raider replied.

"The girl?"

"No," Raider said. "Johnny Welton's father. I don't think he was killed by Indians. Leastways the odds are against it."

"What is your basis for that conclusion?"

"It just don't figure," Raider continued. "There hasn't been any Indian trouble out there since Chief Joseph sent Colonel Nelson packing. That was over two years ago and then up in the Idaho country. It wasn't even a full-fledged war—more of an uprising that came and went."

"That sounds extremely logical," Doc replied.

"Another thing," Raider said. "Welton's spread is in the southern half of the territory. Most of the Indian tribes have moved north onto the reservations near the Canadian border. They haven't caused trouble either."

"You know this firsthand?" Doc asked skeptically.

"Remember when we were in Denver four months ago?" Raider replied. "I played poker with an Indian agent named Clayton. He had a few shots of the hard stuff and started to flap his gums."

"What about the possibility of renegades?"

"Maybe," Raider said. "They were having trouble at the time with a young buck named Wounded Wolf. He was the son of Gray Wolf and the nephew of Chief Joseph. Wounded Wolf wanted to break the treaty and unite the northern tribes. But the tribe kept him on a chain—or that's what Clayton said."

"What tribe does this Wounded Wolf belong to?" Doc asked.

"Sioux," Raider said.

"The same as our Little Bright Wing," Doc said.

"Let's talk to her," Raider urged.

"Soon," Doc replied. "There's something else that bothers me, Raider."

"Cut loose," Raider said.

"Young Welton's aversion to authority rubs me the wrong way," Doc replied. "If he's not a wanted man, why does he dread the idea of facing the law?"

"It's the territory," Raider replied. "We've seen it before, Doc. The frontier don't exactly attract your law-abiding citizens. You been spending too much time in cities."

"But the current territorial governor of Montana has an impeccable reputation as a public servant," Doc offered. "I don't know him personally, but he had supposedly instituted several reforms in his tenure."

"Lot of land out there, Doc," Raider replied. "Sometimes the arm of the law ain't that long."

They sat quietly for a moment, contemplating the facts. Doc had the education, the logical point of view; Raider went on instinct and gut response. Together, they came at the mystery from every angle. There were a hell of a lot of angles, Raider thought.

"You said that you met Jack Welton?" Doc asked.

"I was just a pup back then," Raider replied. "Came out here looking for gold. Damn me if I didn't find some. Not much."

"What were your impressions of the man?" Doc asked.

"I only went hunting with him once."

"Well, if you can't remember..."

"He was big," Raider replied. "As tall as Johnny, but filled out more. Johnny will look like him when he gets a few years on him. He's damned near as tough as his old man."

"You tried the father, too?" Doc asked.

"I was kinda hotheaded back then," Raider offered.

"I'm sure," Doc said. "Do you think Welton was the type of man to be ruled by a woman?"

"You heard the kid's story," Raider replied. "His pa went back to ranching because of his wife's memory haunting him."

"Yes, but that only bespeaks a sentimental streak beneath a rough exterior," Doc replied. "And keep in mind that the new wife couldn't sway him toward throwing in with her brother."

"You don't miss anything, Doc."

"Raider, what is your feeling about this case so far?"

"Somebody gave it to the kid but good," Raider replied. "I think there's dirty business going on."

"Well," Doc said with a smile. "We know how accurate your hunches can be. And it just so happens that I concur."

"We should talk to the Sioux girl."

"I suggest we have Miss Summers present at our questioning," Doc replied.

"The female touch, eh?" Raider said.

"And you must admit, she has earned it," Doc said with a laugh. "She has indeed."

Wrapped in a woolen blanket, Little Bright Wing cowered on the blue satin comforter of her brass bed, glaring like a treed mountain lion at Doc and Raider. Burning, elliptical eyes characterized her oval face. She had thick, pouting lips and hip-length shiny black hair that fell over her shoulders onto her tiny bosom. She was the smallest of Reva's girls. Raider thought she was pretty, even though she wasn't exactly possessed of the healthy proportions he preferred. Doc had no opinion of her beauty as he studied Little Bright Wing.

"Tell us what you know about Jack Welton," Doc said.

The Indian girl was silent.

"Maybe you should let me handle it," Raider said. "I know a little bit more about dealing with squaws."

"I ain't no squaw!" the girl cried.

"You leave your tribe or did your people throw you out?" Raider asked.

"Piss on your mother!" she rejoined.

"Why you little . . ."

Raider grabbed the girl's wrists, but Doc forced him to release his bear-paw grip on her.

"Where did you learn to speak English?" Doc asked.

"You know you speak it very well."

"You have a white pa or a white ma?" Raider asked.

"Chew on a buffalo pie, cowboy," she rasped. "I ain't saying nothing to you or to the dandy."

Raider turned to Reva.

"Send a wire to the Indian agent in Sacramento," Raider said. "Tell him we've got a fugitive squaw and we want to ship her back to the reservation."

"You can't do that!" cried Little Bright Wing.

"I will if Raider tells me to," Reva replied.

"You'll be back on the reservation by the end of the month," Raider said.

"You ever been on a reservation, cowboy?" she said. "Dogs live better in San Francisco. I'd rather be a whore than a squaw. I don't want to live like an Indian."

"But dear girl," Doc said, "you are an Indian."

"No! I was raised by a white soldier and his wife," she said. "My village was attacked when I was just a baby. But the commanding officer wouldn't let his soldiers kill me. He took me to live with him and his wife. I was raised white, but the War Department made my father . . . the soldier, send me back to the tribe three years ago, after the last treaty."

"And so you ran away to become a prostitute," Reva said.

"Sioux braves treat their ponies better than their women," said Little Bright Wing. "You can't send me back there."

"Then cooperate with us and we'll see to it that you're treated properly," Doc said.

"Sure," she replied. "I talk and then you send me back to the reservation."

"I guarantee that we won't do that," Doc said. "In fact, if you want to help us, most likely you'll be set free."

Little Bright Wing glared at Raider.

"Is the dandy lying to me?" she asked.

"I ain't never knowed him to lie to a woman," Raider said.

Little Bright Wing shook her head.

"No," she said. "I don't know anything."

"Yeah, well, then why would Johnny Welton come all the way from Montana if you didn't know something about his father's death?" Raider offered.

She was thinking about it. Raider could see it in her dark, frightened eyes. She knew something and would use it as barter for her freedom. She looked at Doc again.

"You won't send me back to the reservation?" she asked.

"On my word as a Pinkerton," Doc said.

She sighed. "All right, dandy. What do you want to know?"

"Tell us about Sherman Ivery?" Doc asked.

Her eyes grew wider.

"How do you know about him?" she cried.

"The kid told us," Raider said. "Do you know Ivery?"

"Yeah, I know him," she replied.

"What were you to him?" Doc asked.

"What do you think?" she replied hatefully.

She had been his whore, she told them. When she finally ran away from the tribe, she had headed south, aimlessly roaming the ranges. On the fifth day after her escape, she crossed paths with a party of men who had been hunting elk. Sherman Ivery had been the leader of the party. He took her back to his ranch, the place he had lived before he moved into the lodge at the Bar W.

"Did he kill Johnny Welton's father?" Raider asked.

"No!" she insisted.

"You're pretty loyal for a whore," Raider said.

"I know he didn't kill him," she persisted.

"Can you prove it?"

"I saw Jack Welton get murdered!" she blurted out.

"Well," Doc replied. "Now we're getting somewhere. Perhaps we should all compose ourselves and let this girl tell her story."

Little Bright Wing assumed the proud, sullen posture of a defeated warrior. She leaned back, pulling the blanket tighter around her bosom. Looking at her sweet face, Raider would never have believed her capable of lying. But he knew human nature a little better than that.

"I was riding the east ridge the day Jack Welton was shot," she said.

"Ivery let you ride his horses?" Raider said.

"He let me have the run of the place," she replied. "He didn't care what I did as long as I was in his bed at night. I can tell you that his bitch sister didn't like me. No siree. And I hated her too."

"Is the sister a moral sort of person?" Doc asked.

"If you mean a goody-goody, no!" said the Indian girl. "If you ask me, I think she was wanting to tup her brother herself. She was sick in the head."

"We'll take that observation for what it is worth," Doc said. "Tell us about the murder."

"I'm trying!" she shouted. "I told you I was riding the east ridge that day. I was out picking herbs. Ivery was having trouble with me, understand? He didn't always have it when we were in bed. He told me to make him Injun medicine to make him have it again."

"Interesting," Doc said.

"You weren't there, dandy," she replied. "I had to sleep with him. I didn't find any herbs to make him better. I picked things that would put him to sleep so I wouldn't have to touch him."

"Stop pussyfooting," Raider said. "You saw Jack Welton get murdered. Unless you're bulling us."

"I saw him," she replied. "That day he was riding in the valley below me. He was a long way off, but I knew it was him."

"How far?" Doc asked.

"I don't know, maybe a half mile down," the girl replied. "I don't know much about that stuff."

"You sure it was him?" Raider asked.

"Jack Welton was the biggest man I ever seen," she replied. "And he was wearing his fur coat. He always wore it, even in the summer. It had three or four different pelts from his hunting."

"She's right," Raider said. "I remember that coat."

"He was riding below me," Little Bright Wing continued.

"I was walking my horse because the trail was so narrow and rocky. Then he slowed down and stopped. So I stopped too and started watching him. I liked watching him. It was kind of crazy but I liked it."

"Did he do anything out of the ordinary?" Doc asked.

"No, he just got off his horse and kept looking to the north, like he was waiting for someone," she replied. "We were there a little while before five or six men rode in from the north, where he had been watching."

"What did the men do?" Raider asked.

"They just talked to him and rode off in the direction from where they came," she said.

"Was Ivery among them?" Doc asked.

"No, I swear he wasn't," she replied. "I would have recognized him. They weren't men that I had ever seen before."

"Then who killed Welton?" Raider asked.

"I don't know," she replied.

"But you said you saw him get plugged," Raider said.

"I did," she replied. "Later. He just stayed there after the men left, like he was thinking about something. And I watched him until I heard the gun. It was loud. It echoed through the valley. Jack Welton fell to the ground like a dead dog."

"And you didn't get a glimpse of the killer?" Doc asked.

"No, he was somewhere else on the ridge."

"Hold your horehound," Raider said. "You mean you were on the same ridge with the killer and you didn't see him?"

"No, I didn't see anyone."

"What did you do after Welton was shot?" Doc asked.

"I went back to Ivery's ranch house," she replied.

"Did you see anything unusual on the way back?" Doc asked.

"No, not a living soul," she said.

"Didn't you think about helping Welton?" Raider barked.

"He was dead," she said. "Even from the ridge I could tell that. And I don't know what happened to the body."

"What was the situation at Ivery's place when you got back?" Doc asked.

"Everything was calm," she replied. "Sherman had been there all afternoon."

"You can't know that for sure," Raider challenged. "He could have been ahead of you on the ridge."

"Raider has a point," Doc said. "He could have hurried back to the ranch house, preceding you by a few minutes."

"I can tell you that I thought that too," said Little Bright Wing. "I even asked him, but he had been with his friend all afternoon."

"Who was the friend?" Doc asked.

"I don't know," she replied. "Sherman made me leave the room before I could ask."

"What did he look like?"

"He was an old man," she replied. "Dressed all in black, like a preacher. He didn't say anything when he saw me. I was going to tell Sherman about the killing, but I held off until later."

"And what was Ivery's reaction when you told him?" Doc asked.

"It was like he already knew," she replied.

"Hell fire," Raider said. "Ivery's happier than a possum eating peach rinds if he has a preacher to swear he was with him all day. It don't look good."

"It might not necessarily be a preacher," Doc said. "A number of occupations feature black dress. And it could simply be a personal taste of Mr. Ivery's co-conspirator."

Doc leaned in toward Raider and spoke in a whisper.

"Ask her about Wounded Wolf," he said.

Raider turned toward the girl.

"Johnny Welton told us that Indians killed his pa," Raider said. "Did Ivery tell him that?"

"Yes," she replied. "That's when I headed out. I knew the kid would come looking for me."

"Why do you say that?" Doc asked.

"Before I left, the tribe was having a council to decide the fate of my husband," she said. "I know my husband came looking for me. He was seen near the valley, hunting elk with his party of braves. I knew the kid would make the connection."

"What connection?" Raider demanded.

"Ivery told the kid that Wounded Wolf killed his father," she said.

"So?"

"Wounded Wolf is my husband," she said. "The tribe gave him permission to come looking for me, as long as he didn't break the new treaty. Now do you understand why I don't want to go back to the tribe?"

"Most assuredly," Doc replied.

"Can't say as I blame you," Raider chimed in.

"What's it like being married to an Indian?" Reva asked.

"Y'all can talk about that later," Raider replied. "Besides, I ain't sure I want to hear about it."

Little Bright Wing, who was spent from enacting her story, leaned back against the brass frame of the bed. A small sigh escaped from her round mouth. She was exhausted, Doc thought. They probably wouldn't get much more information out of her.

"Thank you, Little Bright Wing," Doc said. "You've been most helpful. Miss Summers, is there a place where Raider and I can talk privately?"

"Why don't you sit on the veranda," Reva replied. "If Wo Hop is still awake, I'll have him bring you some tea."

"Do you have any brandy?" Doc asked.

"Yeah, I could use a shot myself," Raider said.

"Wo Hop will bring you whatever I have," Reva replied.

"Thank you kindly," Raider said, winking at Reva.

Doc turned toward the door with Raider right behind him.

"What about me?" Little Bright Wing called.

"Tie her to the bed," Doc said to Reva.

"You promised to let me go," the Indian girl protested.

"We only promised that you wouldn't be sent back to the reservation," Doc replied. "Don't fret, girl. We'll probably release you eventually. But for now, I want you to remain nearby. I may have to ask you some more questions."

"Tup your mother, you dandy bastard," cried Little Bright Wing.

"Damned if she ain't got some mouth on her," Raider said. "I ain't never heard no woman talk like that. Not even a savage!"

They left the room with Little Bright Wing calling after them with all varieties of profanity. Downstairs, the main parlor was empty, as were most of the rooms above. It had been one hell of a night at Reva's, Raider thought. When they emerged onto the veranda, the air was cool and refreshing. Morning birds were starting to sing in the scattering of trees. It would be daylight soon. They settled into a pair of wooden chairs. Raider put his boots up on the railing of the porch, while Doc torched the end of another cheroot with a sulfur match.

"I must say that you've happened onto a rather complex case, Raider," Doc said, taking the lead.

"Something, ain't it?" Raider replied. "Hell, we ain't even in the territory and already we got more information than we know what to do with."

Behind them, Wo Hop stumbled sleepily onto the veranda, growling beneath his breath. He slammed a tray next to Doc and then disappeared back into the house. Doc poured two glasses of brandy. Raider eyed the shot of brown liquid.

"No red-eye?" Raider asked.

"I know you hate the finer things in life, Raider, but this brandy is all we have," Doc replied.

"What the hell?" Raider said. "Hooch is hooch."

The brandy burned his throat as Raider downed the shot in one gulp. Doc, ignoring Raider's lack of sophistication, rolled his glass around in his hands, slowly sipping the fine liquor. They were silent as the whiskey glow spread over them, smoothing out the rough edges left over from the long night. Raider finally found the starting point.

"You think Little Bright Wing is telling the truth about Jack Welton's murder?" Raider asked.

"She might be lying to protect her husband, Wounded

Wolf," Doc replied.

"She don't seem to care two hoots about him," Raider offered.

"No, she doesn't," Doc replied. "Nor does she care about her former...shall we say, employer, Mr. Ivery. That's why her story rings true to me. Although she's certainly quick enough to invent such an unlikely tale."

"Looks like we have to talk to a man named Sherman Ivery," Raider said. "I bet he won't be happy to see us."

"Yes," Doc replied. "You could be right. Hmm..."

"Something bothering you, Doc?"

"Everything pointing to Ivery," Doc replied. "It all fits together too well. What do you make of the mysterious preacher in black?"

"Could be anybody," Raider said. "If Ivery's got hired men around, he could pay one of them to say he was at home when Jack Welton was killed by Indians."

"Yes, but if things are as lawless out there as you say, then why would Ivery even bother with an alibi?"

"You got to admit, he don't seem too worried about covering his tracks," Raider replied.

"Exactly," Doc said. "He let Little Bright Wing escape."

"Maybe he wanted Welton to follow her," Raider replied. "Don't worry, Doc. A careless man will be easy to catch."

Doc shifted in his chair, pouring another glass of brandy. Reva had not supplied him with a snifter, but the brandy itself was fine Cognac. A pleasure to the refined palate and a stimulant to the probing mind.

"There are two key elements that we cannot ignore," Doc said finally.

"Fire away," Raider replied.

"First, we'll have to question the legality of the documents giving Velma Ivery Welton the inheritance of the ranch," he replied. "Secondly, we must ascertain her involvement in her brother's scheme."

"Don't look like she had too much to do with it," Raider said.

"That remains to be seen," Doc replied. "We do know that she tried to sway Jack Welton into a partnership with her brother, and that she wasn't upset when the partnership was denied."

"Don't forget, they tossed Johnny out," Raider said.

"Yes, but they allowed the sister to stay," Doc replied. "I wonder how much the sister's moral nature played a part in that?"

"I wonder if she really loved the old man?"

"Hmm," Doc said. "Young Welton's plight reminds me a bit of Shakespeare's Hamlet. The unscrupulous brother, the weak wife. A deposed prince."

"Well, I don't know nothin' about that," Raider replied. "But Johnny sure as hell has his head in the mountain lion's mouth."

"Everything is purely speculation now," Doc said. "We'll have to be in the field to determine all the facts."

"What are we going to do with the girl?"

"That remains to be seen," Doc replied. "We'll have to decide before we leave tomorrow."

"Think we'll catch hell from the boss?" Raider asked.

"Doubtful. We are authorized to accept a case that falls into our area of expertise. This case fits all our guidelines. A common murder investigation wherein the authorities have failed to find the killer. And as long as Johnny Welton wires a retainer to the home office, what can Mr. Pinkerton say to us? You know, Raider, I hardly think—"

"Shh," Raider said.

"What is it?"

Raider sat up suddenly, pulling his feet off the railing, turning to his right as though he'd sensed a shifting in the cool air. A rustling at the corner of the veranda had caught his attention. Shuffling feet followed the rustling on the wooden deck. A dark body, reflected in the shadows, moved toward them.

"Git low, Doc," Raider said.

Raider dived out of the chair, hit the porch deck, and rolled as he fished the .44 from his holster. He cocked the hammer and aimed at the shadow, expecting another attack. His voice boomed out, stopping the shadowy figure in his tracks.

"Take another step and you'll be talking from the back of your head, partner."

"It's me, cowboy. Don't shoot!"

Raider was on his feet in an instant. Johnny Welton moved into the light. Raider kept the pistol trained on him. He wasn't taking any chances. Doc may have trusted the kid, but Raider had seen him holding a rifle to the whore's head.

"You always so trigger happy?" Johnny said to Raider.

"Only when I been up all night, chasing savages and fighting in the streets," Raider replied. "I got a right to be jumpy, boy."

"Why don't you put the hog's leg back in your holster," Johnny replied.

"I'll hold the pistol on you until you convince me that you weren't slipping off by yourself," Raider replied.

"I was coming to see the dandy," said Johnny Welton.

Doc was on his feet, brushing the dust from his new suit.

"Mr. Welton," said Doc, "never call me a *dandy* again. You may call me Doc, or Mr. Weatherbee, or *Dr*. Weatherbee—but please, no more allusions to my habits or my manners."

"Y'all sure are touchy," Johnny said.

"Forgive us," Doc replied. "We lead rather harrowing lives. Now, what did you have on your mind, Johnny?"

"I want to talk to the girl," he said seriously.

"We did," Doc replied. "She holds that your father was not killed by Indians, but by a rifle shot from the east ridge of the Bar W—your ranch, I believe."

"I knew it!" Johnny cried. "Ivery."

"She claims Ivery didn't do it either," Raider said.

"She's lying," Johnny replied.

"Maybe," Raider said. "But what if she's telling the truth?"

"I know the truth," Johnny insisted. "Ivery killed my pa."

"You're paying us to find out the truth," Doc said. "Raider and I are going with you to the Montana Territory. We're pulling out tomorrow."

"Just give me five minutes with the girl," Johnny replied. "I'll get her to tell the truth."

"I suggest you answer a few questions for us," Doc said.

"Not unless I talk to the girl."

"Sit down, boy," Raider said, reminding him of the .44.

Reluctantly, Johnny Welton slouched down into Raider's wooden chair. They gave him a few minutes to cool down. The porch was starting to glow purple in the predawn. Raider thought the kid's sallow face looked spooky in the weird light. After another glass of brandy, Doc started in again.

"Johnny, Little Bright Wing said that she never saw your father's body after she left the ridge. Did *you* ever see the dead body of your father?"

"No," Johnny replied. "Ivery told me that there wasn't anything left after the Indians bushwacked him."

"No *corpus delecti,*" Doc muttered. "Murder will be hard to prove in the absence of a corpse."

"Little Bright Wing was a witness," Raider said.

"She's hardly reputable," Doc said. "No, we have to find the body of Jack Welton. That will be our number-one priority when we reach the territory."

Johnny leaned back in the chair, staring out at the street. He was thinking about something from his childhood, maybe. Tears pooled in his eyes, but he fought them back, not letting them run down his face. The kid was strong, inside and out, Raider thought.

"Was there something else on your mind?" Doc asked.

"Just this," Johnny replied.

He reached into his pocket and pulled out a dirty ball of cloth that had been wrapped around something in the middle. Doc took the crumpled ball from Johnny's hand and spread it open in his own palm. A key shined on the oily cloth.

"Where did you get this?" Doc asked.

"My sister gave it to me right before I left Elk Lodge," he replied. "I found it in my saddlebag with a note."

"What did the note say?" Raider asked.

"Just, 'Pa left this behind for you, Johnny.' Nothing else. I can't figure out what it means. I don't think Diana even knew what it was for."

"No, or she would have included an explanation in the note," Doc replied.

He turned the key between his fingers, examining it in the growing light. After a moment, he handed it to Raider, who gave it a quick inspection. They both knew what it was.

"Strongbox key," Raider said. "Probably Wells Fargo."

"Agreed," Doc said.

"Why would Pa have a strongbox?"

"Obviously to protect something of value," Doc replied. "But I doubt that he stored it at the ranch."

"Then where?" Johnny asked.

"Raider?" Doc said.

"I'd guess a Wells Fargo office," Raider replied. "There's a number on the key. It has to match up somewhere."

"A bank, perhaps," Doc offered.

"Nearest bank is Helena," Johnny said. "Wells Fargo too."

"I suggest we—"

"What the hell?"

Muzzle flashes from a rifle barked on a rooftop across the street from Reva's place. Lead slugs slammed into the wall behind Johnny Welton's head. The three of them went belly down on the porch. The rifle was quiet for a second.

"He's reloading," Raider said, drawing his .44.

"I mark him on the roof of the blue house," Doc said. "Just behind the branches of that overhanging tree."

They peered between the slats of the veranda railing.

"He was shooting at me!" Johnny cried.

"Think he's gone?" Raider said.

Doc kicked one of the chairs with his heel, sending it across the veranda toward the front steps. As soon as the chair hit the top step, the rifle belched fire again and lead chopped the chair into splinters. Raider returned fire with the .44, but the sniper was out of range for anything but a lucky shot.

"He's got his bearings now," Raider said. "And I can't hit him from here. Not with this."

"He must want Johnny pretty badly to risk shooting him here," Doc said.

"You ain't gonna get me, Ivery!" Johnny cried.

The rifle chattered again, kicking up splints of wood all around them.

"He's got a repeater," Raider said. "Probably thirty caliber."

"Would you like to suggest a course of action?" Doc asked.

"Ain't but one way," Raider said. "You draw his fire while I move. Wait about three minutes and draw his fire again. I'll put a little surprise on him."

Doc kicked the other chair, evoking a response from the repeating rifle. When the .30-caliber music began, Raider danced to his feet and dove headlong through an open window into Miss Reva's parlor. She was standing at the top of the stairs, holding the neck of her nightgown.

"Not again," she cried.

"Keep still, honey," Raider said. "I'm gonna take care of it pronto."

He bounded up the stairs, past his mistress. The Sharps was in Reva's room, under the bed. Raider found it and slid the .50-caliber cartridge into the rolling breech. The rifle had to be cocked before it could be loaded.

"What are you going to do with that?" Reva asked.

But he ignored her as he bolted back down the stairs and then began to circle through the house to the rear steps. Reva kept a tall ladder out back, for men who wanted to slip away from an untimely visit by a constable or an irate wife. Raider leaned the ladder against the house and climbed with the heavy Sharps balanced in one hand.

"Be careful, honey," Reva called from below.

Raider crawled across the roof to the front edge of the house. He was above Doc and Johnny on a flat portion of the roof structure. From his vantage point, he could see the roof of the blue house. The assassin was a shadow between the branches of the tree, like a gobbler turkey hiding in the swamp. Raider could see the glimmer from a stovepipe hat on the sniper's head. Like Abe Lincoln, he thought.

"I got you now, boy," he muttered.

A clamor resounded from the veranda. The repeating rifle erupted again. Doc was right on time below. Raider rested the Sharps on the roof, using a dent in the rain gutter to steady the barrel. His fingers raised the calibrated sight. He set the distance. As he sighted in on the man's stovepipe hat, he dropped the bead to compensate for the downward angle. If the rifle aimed true, the slug would catch him in the chest. High or low—well, he thought, it didn't matter as long as he hit him. The .50-caliber slug would take care of the rest.

"So long, scalawag," Raider said.

The Sharps thundered like the breath of Jove from the heavens. The recoil moved Raider back a little. When he crawled to the edge of the roof, he could see that the figure was no longer visible in the branches of the tree. Instead, the body was stretched out on the rooftop. And even with his limited vision, Raider could see that there was no head between the neck and the stovepipe hat a few feet away from the corpse.

CHAPTER FOUR

On the roof of what turned out to be an abandoned house, Doc hovered over the decapitated body. The man was wearing an old Civil War blue uniform jacket with stiff, stained buckskin pants. The stovepipe hat had rolled into a corner of the roof. Johnny came up behind Doc and looked over his shoulder at the remains of Raider's handiwork. Raider and his weak stomach could not have cared less about the bloody residue.

"This son of a bitch tried to kill me," said Johnny. "You sure gave this peckerwood a headache, Mr. Raider."

"Hell, Doc," Raider replied. "Why'd you have to come up here anyway? The constable's probably on the way. Some citizen is bound to go for the law after this ruckus."

"He's right," Johnny said. "Maybe we should—"

"Someone wants you dead," Doc rejoined. "I'd like a chance to look around, before the amateurs come in here and rearrange everything. We have to find out who tried to kill you."

"Ivery!" Johnny said. "That's why he let the girl leave, so I'd follow her and he could send this bushwhacker after me."

Doc reached into the man's coat pocket and pulled out a bag of coins. Five twenty-dollar gold pieces—double eagles—fell out into his hand. Someone had paid a hundred dollars to have Johnny Welton killed.

"He certainly must have considerable resources," Doc said. "There are men around who would kill you for much less."

"I can't figure out why he went after Johnny *here*," Raider said. "He could have taken him in more open ground, out of the city."

"He probably just caught up to me," Johnny replied. "I move fast on the range. And it took me three days to find the girl once I got here."

"How did you find her?" Doc asked.

"Don't have to pay much to get a whore talking," Johnny replied. "I knew what Little Bright Wing would do when she got to the city. I used part of the money left from selling the cows to the miners to work my way around."

"Ingenious," Doc replied.

"There ain't much more here," Raider chimed in.

He wouldn't look at the corpse.

"His hat is over there," he said, pointing to the corner.

"Let me see that," Johnny replied.

Raider stepped across the roof and picked up the crimson-stained stovepipe hat. He tossed it to Johnny, who examined it and then threw it on the dead man's chest. Raider flinched when Johnny kicked the body in the side.

"This son of bitch was working for Ivery," Johnny said. "I saw him at the ranch the last time I was there."

"How can you be sure?" Raider asked.

"The hat," Johnny replied. "I'd know it anywhere. Even if the cowboy knocked out his face."

"Your rifle shoots high!" Raider snapped. "I was aiming for his chest."

"I'm glad you killed him," Johnny replied. "This ol' boy wasn't counting on you, Mr. Raider."

"That's enough," Raider replied.

He always felt nauseous after he killed someone. He didn't like it, even when the person needed killing. Raider was afraid it would all come back on him one day, even though he had only killed people he had had to kill.

"The law's on us!" Johnny said suddenly in a hoarse whisper.

Two shiny-buttoned constables—a mustached Irish sergeant and a young patrol officer—emerged onto the roof. It hadn't taken as long as Doc had thought it would for them to get there. The Sharps had shaken up the local authorities. Such a thunder clap could not go unnoticed, even in such a rough section of town. Doc rose from his inspection of the body, heading to meet the policemen with his hand outstretched. The sergeant and the officer refused to shake his hand.

"What's the disturbance?" the sergeant asked.

"There's been a killing," Doc replied nonchalantly.

"I thought there had been an explosion," the officer said.

"No, it was the report of a Sharps fifty-caliber rifle," Doc replied. "I believe it is often referred to as a buffalo gun."

He gestured toward Raider in a grand style.

"My friend there, the tall, rough-looking gentleman, shot the head off that unfortunate ruffian on the deck," Doc continued. "As you can see, if you will step closer, the slug blew off the man's entire cranial enclosure at the neck. You'll probably find what's left of the head at the bottom of the back alley."

The younger officer ran out immediately, holding his hand over his mouth. The sergeant took a long look at the body, twirling the end of his bright orange mustache. Then he glanced at Raider, who still rested his hand on the butt of his holstered .44.

"You killed him?" the sergeant asked.

"He was shooting at our friend here," Raider replied.

"All right, what the hell is going on here?" the sergeant asked.

"Allow me," Doc said. "My name is Weatherbee, and this is my partner, Raider. We are employed by the Pinkerton National Detective Agency, and at the present moment we are charged with the protection of this young gentleman.

His name is Johnny Welton. The man lying there made an attempt on our lives. My partner simply replied with his own forceful methods."

"You got something to prove you're Pinkertons?" the sergeant demanded.

Doc produced their credentials from his coat pocket. The sergeant nervously rubbed his mustache as he contemplated the situation. Doc decided the best thing to do was to make things easy for the constable.

"Of course, you can detain us if you wish," Doc continued. "We'll be happy to comply. As Mr. Welton's life seems to be in jeopardy, I would like nothing better than to put him under the protection of the San Francisco constabulary."

"I ain't going with no—"

Raider dug his elbow into Johnny's ribs, silencing his protest. Doc was handling the law just fine. Nobody could outtalk Doc. He was as smooth as the snake in the Garden of Eden. And almost as easy to get along with.

"Pinkertons, eh?" the sergeant said. "You willing to sign something about all of this?"

"Immediately," Doc replied. "And we will register a complete report with our own office, as is our usual procedure. You are welcome to the contents of that report. I'll give you the address of our office in Chicago. We have a reputation for cooperation to the letter of the law."

The sergeant eyed them over, wondering if he was being taken. He looked back down at the body and nudged it a little with his foot. Flies were starting to light on the bloody stump of the neck. Some way to start up a Sunday, the sergeant thought.

"You sure he shot first?" the sergeant asked.

"He had us pinned down for ten minutes," Raider replied.

"You sure corked him," the sergeant said with a macabre chuckle. "Hell, I ain't never seen him around here before. Did he have anything on him?"

"Just this bag of gold coins," Doc said, extending the pouch to the sergeant. "Of course, you must take this with you, in the event that his relatives call for his belongings."

"Yes," the sergeant said, glancing over his shoulder to see if the young constable was still downstairs. "Maybe we shouldn't mention the money in our reports."

"That's up to you," Doc replied. "Of course, we could let this entire matter drop completely. I could certainly do without the extra paperwork."

The sergeant rubbed his chin, slipping the bag of double eagles into his pocket.

"No reason to stir up the Citizens Committee," the sergeant said.

"Especially with the election year upcoming," Doc said.

"If you weren't Pinkertons, I'd have to take you in," the sergeant said. "But you told me everything I wanted to know. Maybe you should just clear out."

"An excellent idea," Doc called as the sergeant began to make his way from the roof.

Doc had talked them out of trouble again, Raider thought.

"You got the devil's tongue, Mr. Weatherbee," Johnny said.

"He delivered us this time," Raider rejoined. "But I got a sneaking feeling that we're gonna find a lot of trouble up the road."

Doc and Johnny were suddenly quiet.

"I ain't climbing that goddamn pole, Doc," Raider said. "Let the kid do it. He's spry and willing."

"Raider," Doc replied. "Let's not have this argument again. Johnny doesn't know how to hook up the wires. You do. And the sooner you do it, the sooner we get on our way."

Raider looked up the telegraph pole and shook his head. Doc wanted to get a message to Wagner, their immediate supervisor in the home office. They were a day out of San Francisco, traveling southwest for a reason only Doc knew. The party had left the same day Raider had killed the man on the roof. It followed that they had to report their movements. They could not operate without the knowledge of the home office.

"Just climb the pole, Raider," Doc said. "The longer you put it off, the longer we have to stay by the side of this godforsaken clay road."

Doc had opened the floor of his Studebaker wagon, pulling up the compartment that hid his telegraph key and gravity batteries. Raider really didn't like the contraption. It made him feel all crawly inside. It wasn't natural to be in touch with people so far away, especially so fast and easy. When Doc reported in, Raider felt like someone was spying on him. Still, Doc was right. They had to check in. It was the proper procedure.

"Can't we send a wire when we reach another town?" Raider asked.

"This will be quicker," Doc replied. "And we're right by the line."

"Aw right, give me the wire," Raider said. "But you better send everything. I ain't climbing another pole on this trip."

Raider tried to be careful when he shinnied up the pole, but he caught splinters anyway. By the time he hooked up the wires and shinnied back down, he was plenty mad. Sometimes Doc's toys could be a real nuisance.

"Thank you," Doc said. "I'll give you a tincture for your splinters when I'm through. Do you think you can survive until then?"

"Just don't ask me to feed that mule," Raider shot back.

"Can I watch you work that telegraph key?" asked Johnny Welton.

"Yes," Doc replied. "But don't get in the way."

"It's real exciting, kid," Raider said. "But you better watch it. Ol' Doc there might kill you explaining how that thing works."

"Don't you ever shut your mouth, cowboy?"

Raider looked up at Little Bright Wing, who was sitting on Johnny Welton's horse. She had been riding with Doc on the wagon, before he had decided to use his telegraph key. Doc had also suggested that they take her along. He thought she might aid them in the investigation of Jack Welton's murder.

Doc had tricked Little Bright Wing into coming along. Instead of forcing her to ride with them, he had simply told her she was free to go. Reva promptly dismissed her from the house. At first Little Bright Wing had been thrilled to have her freedom, but when she realized she had no other place to go, she told Doc and Raider she wanted to ride with them for a ways. Doc staunchly refused, which prompted Little Bright Wing to follow them down the street, cursing at the top of her tiny lungs. Doc then allowed her to ride on his wagon, with the promise that she would not make trouble.

"Where'd you get that mouth?" Raider asked. "Is that the same mouth you use to kiss your momma?"

"My momma used to work with yours in a whorehouse," she replied. "That's where you were born, with a cowboy's dick in your ass."

"I surrender," Raider said. "I can't outcuss you, girl."

"I hate you, cowboy," she railed.

"Aw, you're just mad 'cause I wouldn't let you into my bedroll last night," Raider replied.

"I wanted to keep warm," replied Little Bright Wing.

"Too bad," Raider muttered.

"You're just afraid of Reva," she cried. "She's got you pussy-whipped. Well, I can tell you that I'm not one of her girls anymore. So if you want it from me, just let me sleep in your bedroll with you. I'll give it to you to keep from freezing my ass."

"Just shut your trap," Raider replied.

She didn't know how much she was tempting him with the offer. Raider already missed the warm sheets at Reva's. He also missed what happened between them—waking next to Reva, taking her when he wanted her. She had been a wildcat on the afternoon before they left, after Raider had killed the man in the stovepipe hat. She had never been more eager, out of breath, and wet as the morning grass. She couldn't wait for him to get inside. All of the excitement had gotten to her.

"Cowboy," Little Bright Wing said, interrupting his reverie. "What's the dandy doing?"

"His name is Doc and my name is Raider," he replied. "And he's sending a message to Chicago."

"Bullshit," she replied. "He can't do that. Can he?"

"That man is a wizard," Raider replied. "He's like a witch. He can turn you into a pile of ashes if he wants to."

"I ain't sleeping with him," she said.

Raider turned back to see Doc completing his message. He waited for the message-received signal and then waved to Raider to climb back up the pole. As Raider reluctantly started forward, Johnny Welton volunteered to take his place. He was captivated by Doc's machinery and wanted desperately to be part of the procedure.

"I can unhook it," Johnny said. "I watched Raider do it."

"Hell, let him try," Raider said.

"Be careful," Doc said. "Sometimes you can receive a mild shock. It won't hurt you, but it might affect your muscle control."

Johnny went up the pole with a quickness that made Raider long for his unscarred youth. Johnny disconnected the wire, but, true to Doc's warning, he felt a mild bit of current tingling through his fingers. He released his grip, and his gangly body plummeted earthward, landing in a tuft of brush at the roadside. Luckily, he didn't break anything.

"I never felt nothing like that before," Johnny said, rubbing his hands. "What was it?"

"Electricity," Doc replied. "I'll explain later."

"He'll probably explain for hours," Raider said, "now you've got him going."

"Let's move out," Doc said.

"How much longer are we gonna travel south?" Johnny asked.

"Southwest," Doc replied. "I suppose I should inform you of the itinerary. First, we are traveling in this direction because we are going to Stockton. From there, I want to transfer to a train which will take us north into Nevada and then Utah."

"Why didn't we just travel by train from Frisco?" Johnny asked.

"Because I want to see if we're being followed," Doc replied. "If Ivery has employed one agent, then he might have more watching for us. Later today, Raider will double back and see if we have anyone on our tail. He's quite good at that."

"Yeah, I've noticed he's sneaky," said Little Bright Wing.

"I suggest that we adopt disguises," Doc replied. "Of course I'll be the traveling apothecary. Johnny, you can be a trapper."

"What about me?" asked Little Bright Wing.

"You and Raider can pose as man and wife," Doc replied. "You can say that you're heading to the Idaho country, to farm and to raise sheep."

"Sheep?" Raider said warily.

"Do you have a better suggestion?" Doc offered.

Little Bright Wing laughed.

"Man and wife, cowboy," she said. "Now maybe you'll let me share your bedroll. That way I won't be cold as hell all the way."

"Don't worry, dear girl," Doc said. "If you get cold, you can sleep next to Judith."

"Judith?"

"His mule." Raider guffawed. "Damn it all, Doc, once in a while you get off a good one."

"No thanks to your mule," said Little Bright Wing. "I'll take the cowboy. He don't smell nearly as bad."

"Don't bet on it," Raider said. "You ain't coming near me."

As Doc had requested in his wire to the home office, their back pay and expenses were forwarded to the Stockton telegraph office, with the authorization to accept Johnny Welton as a client. Doc, in turn, wired the retainer to Wagner while Raider complained about the expenses that had been disallowed in his report. Doc politely pointed out that breaking up a saloon while apprehending a suspect might not constitute an expense in the eyes of the agency.

"It still feels good to have a pocketful of money, even if there ain't much to spend it on," Raider said.

"Our expenses for this assignment could be considerable before we're finished," Doc said. "Take, for instance, your costumes. . . ."

He sent Johnny and Raider in different directions, with general instructions on what to purchase, leaving a little room for their personal imagination and taste. He kept Little Bright Wing with him to keep her from running off on her own. For her he chose a bright calico dress, which was the only dress in her size, and luckily a bargain at two dollars. Cornstarch would lighten her complexion, and a blue bonnet would hide her long black hair. Next to Raider, she would appear to be a diminutive farm girl.

Raider abandoned his Stetson (which would be stored with the rest of his gear in Doc's wagon) for a straw hat and a brown flannel shirt. When choosing a pair of pants, he found that overalls had more pockets to hide knives and the small .35-caliber derringer that even Doc didn't know about. Raider never liked to be unarmed. Too many good men had died with their guard down. Raider at least wanted to go out blasting if someone caught him flat-footed.

Johnny Welton somehow managed to procure another set of buckskins which were newer and less smelly than the ones he had worn into Reva's. The kid seemed to come alive again when he felt the soft leather next to his hide. It was like he had come home after a long time away.

"You look like an Injun scout," Raider said.

"I can't stand civilized clothes," Johnny replied. "They make me feel weak."

"A couple of days in the saddle and you'll be strong enough," Raider said.

"Hey, what about me?" said Little Bright Wing. "Don't I look good, husband?"

"You ain't gettin' no compliments out of me," Raider replied.

"Do I have to travel with this jackass?" she scowled.

"Yes, but it's very important that we don't make any contact with each other until we reach Salt Lake City," Doc said.

"You really think all this sneaking around is necessary?" Raider said.

"We're dealing with an opponent who reached out from the wilds of the Montana Territory," Doc replied. "If he could attempt to kill Johnny in San Francisco, he could try again before we get to Utah. Besides, gossip reaches the ears of a traveling apothecary much faster than the ears of a detective."

"Hey, we gotta sell the horses," Raider said. "I didn't think of that."

"Fortunately, I did," Doc replied. "It won't be necessary to sell the animals. Our train is pulling an empty livestock car. I simply have to make arrangements with the conductor."

"What about your wagon?" Johnny asked.

"Flatcar," Doc replied.

"Then let's get going," Johnny said.

"Steady, boy," Raider replied. "Ivery ain't goin' nowhere. He's comfortable right where he is."

"Maybe, but he's gonna be out of the valley by the end of the month," Johnny said.

"Why then?" Doc asked.

"Winter," Johnny replied. "He plans to drive those cows south before the first snow. If he doesn't get them out by then, he'll lose them."

"But it's only the third of September," Raider offered.

"The first year my Pa was a rancher, he waited until the middle of October to round up his herd," Johnny replied. "The pass got snowed in and he lost most of his cows. The next year, he started the roundup on October first. Hell, that old northwester came screaming down from Canada on us. Must of dropped a foot of snow."

"Damn!" Raider said.

"Winters ain't kind in the territory," Johnny said.

"Ah, but this could work to our advantage," Doc said.

"How's that?" Johnny asked.

"If Ivery is preoccupied with the roundup, he won't have time to cover his tracks," Doc replied. "A man in a hurry is bound to slip eventually."

"So you finally admit that Ivery's the man," Johnny said.

"I admit nothing," Doc rejoined. "I simply hold that Ivery will be the focal point of our investigation."

A train whistle blasted as the engine pulled into the Stockton station.

"We'd better hurry," Doc said. "I have to check with the conductor about the livestock car. They weren't expecting to transport any horses, but the right kind of persuasion could alleviate any misunderstandings."

"Hey, dandy," said Little Bright Wing. "Don't you have any of those fancy words to tell me how beautiful I look?"

"Little Bright Wing, you are a vision," he replied. "I'd run through fire for thy sweet sake. Oh, and from now on, your name will be Mary. Raider, yours should be Joseph."

"Right out of the Good Book," Raider said.

"It wouldn't hurt to have the Deity on our side," Doc said.

He headed off to make arrangements for the horses and his wagon. Raider wondered what Doc would do if anything ever happened to that broken-down mule and the rattling rig. Doc had been crazy in Oregon when he'd had to leave his wagon behind.

"Oh, Joseph, honey," said Little Bright Wing, resting her head on Raider's arm. "I can't wait to start dirt-farming with the man I love. It's God's own land that will keep us alive. Praise be and hallelujah."

"Cork that shit right now," Raider said. "Doc don't want us attracting no attention."

"Piss in your overalls, clodhopper," Little Bright Wing snapped.

"A good wife is obedient and silent," Johnny said. "My Pa used to say that."

"Piss in your buckskins, buffalo stink," Little Bright Wing said. "All of you can go straight to hell."

Raider rolled his eyes, hoping that there were no ladies on the train. Johnny was glad he wouldn't have to travel with Raider and the girl. The journey was going to be long enough without listening to the two of them.

CHAPTER FIVE

Raider was glad when the Rockies were finally behind them. He was never quite prepared for the majestic, jutting peaks that split the territory in half. Doc's wagon had been a royal pain, even though Johnny had taken them through passes where the going was easy for the most part. Johnny was a good guide. He steered them through pass after pass, until the foothills sloped downward into the high, western forests of Montana. After the lichen-covered rocks and boulders, the trees looked damned good to Raider.

"You done good, Johnny," Raider said.

"I been coming through here since I was a boy," Johnny replied. "Good hunting down in these woods. Might pick up a mule deer or an elk. Once in a while a moose wanders down from the north."

"I wouldn't mind a little fresh meat," Raider said.

"I find game to be slightly strong-tasting," Doc replied.

"You would," said a derisive Little Bright Wing.

Her presence had been a temptation for all of them—even Doc. In the close quarters of the mountains, she had offered to share anyone's bedroll, but they had all refused. So she had begun testing their mettle, especially Doc, who proved to be very adaptable, much to her disappointment. Still, she barbed him every chance she got. She figured that

Johnny or Raider would cuff her, so she picked on Doc. Raider sort of admired the way Doc took it in stride.

"I don't know why I came back with you," she said. "You're a bunch of sissies."

"Raider," Doc said with a straight face. "Perhaps we should stake out Little Bright Wing for grizzly bait."

"Nah, she'd scare off a damned wolverine," Raider replied.

"Go ahead and laugh," she cried. "When we come to town, I'm leaving you for good."

As they started into the stunted, elfin firs of the high forests, Johnny didn't tell her there were no towns between them and the Elk Lodge Valley. Once they were through the forests, there were only rolling plains and the smaller ranges. And they still had a ways to go at that.

"You wanna make early camp and do some hunting?" Raider asked. "I'd like to try the Sharps again."

"A fifty-caliber slug for a deer?" Johnny said.

"We might see a moose," Raider said, grinning sheepishly. "And with that cannon of yours, we don't even have to get close."

"Hell, you must want to kill it and field-dress it with one shot," Johnny replied.

"Shut up," said Little Bright Wing. "You're making me sick with all of this killing talk."

"That's bullshit," Johnny said. "Sioux make their women chew their hides, to make them soft on the inside. You've seen more dead animals than me."

"I don't have to be reminded," she said. "It will be a cold day in hell before I go back to the tribe."

The ground sloped downward as the trees became higher. A rough road was cut, but thick brush still grew in the trail. Doc had to take it slower with the Studebaker. Johnny and Raider plodded along next to him.

"Maybe we should ride ahead," Johnny said. "I know a clearing about five miles up. There's usually a herd feeding there. And it wouldn't be a bad place to camp."

"What about Doc?" Raider said.

"He can follow," Johnny replied. "I doubt there'll be any trouble. It's gonna take him a couple of hours to catch up with us."

"That okay with you, Doc?" Raider asked.

"I don't see why not," Doc replied. "My only request is that you shoot a domestic steer, a fat one with a prime fillet."

Raider spurred his mount, an Appaloosa gelding that bolted through the cool air of the forest. Johnny was right behind on his chestnut filly. They wound through the trail, putting some distance between them and Doc. Shafts of light streaked through tall firs—junipers and ponderosa pines—lighting their dusty way.

Raider slowed down after twenty minutes, allowing Johnny to pass him. Johnny knew where they were heading, so Raider let him take the lead. Johnny's mare flew around a bend in the trail, disappearing momentarily. When Raider came around the bend himself, Johnny was standing on the trail, looking down at the ground.

"Fresh tracks," he said. "You got your rifle ready?"

"I want to try the Sharps again," Raider replied.

"It's only one shot," Johnny said. "Don't you have a repeater?"

"I only need one shot," Raider replied.

"All right, let's get to it."

Johnny led his horse into the trees on a path that was less than a foot wide. Raider dismounted and followed him. As they trod through the underbrush, the light seemed to get brighter. They finally burst through the trees onto a rocky precipice that overlooked a deep ravine. They tied their horses and peered over the edge.

"Just like I thought," Johnny said. "Three bucks and five does. See the spikes on the young bucks? The daddy's the one with the big rack."

"He must be a twelve-pointer," Raider said.

The small herd was lying up in the shade of the misshapen trees that curled out of the rocks. Mule deer were a lot bigger than the whitetails back home, Raider thought. He went back to Johnny's mare and loaded the Sharps.

"Take one of the spikes," Johnny said. "No need to kill a doe or that big buck."

"That big un sure would make a good trophy," Raider replied.

"You want trophy or meat?" Johnny said. "The spike buck will be tender. Besides, that big buck is too pretty to kill."

The kid had respect, Raider thought. He found a forked stick and wedged it in a crack, using the rest to steady his aim. Just as he was about to squeeze off, the buck fell to the ground. The two spike bucks bolted, followed by the does, one of which fell a few feet away from the buck into the white-frothed stream that flowed along the bottom of the ravine.

"What the hell?" Raider said.

"Be quiet," Johnny replied nervously. "We've got company."

The soft clodding of unshod hooves reverberated through the slopes of the ravine, the only sound to announce the arrival of an Indian hunting party. Three braves came down out of the trees to claim the fallen deer. Johnny could see the rest of the party, seven or eight braves, tending their ponies in the forest on the other side of the ravine. A tall brave with corded arms and a massive chest leaned over to pick up the buck. He hoisted it onto his shoulders with one quick movement. He was the biggest damned Indian Raider had ever seen.

Behind them, one of the horses snorted. Without a word, the tall brave lifted his arm. The rest of the party stopped. They gazed up the slope, straight at the ledge where Johnny and Raider lay hidden. From their vantage point, Raider and Johnny had the edge with their rifles. It could still be a bloody fight, Raider thought.

The tall brave turned to his party, motioning them back up the slope into the woods. Johnny could see the flashes of color as the hunting party strung up the deer carcasses, field-dressing them, stripping the hides and loading the meat onto a travois. The process was quick, and the party was on their way after ten minutes.

"That son of a bitch snaked our kill," Raider said.

"Yeah, well, he could have snaked a lot more than that," Johnny replied. "That was Wounded Wolf himself, partner."

"No lie?"

"None other."

"He's about the meanest-looking Injun I ever saw," Raider said.

"He knew we were here," Johnny replied. "He just didn't feel like fucking with us today. We'd be in trouble if he finds out we got the woman with us."

"I wonder what he's doing down this far?" Raider said. "You think he's still after Little Bright Wing?"

"He's heading north," Johnny replied. "Most likely, he's just come too far south with his hunting party. This forest is easy for him to hunt 'cause there ain't no settlements nearabouts."

"Think he's going home?" Raider asked.

"Probably," Johnny replied. "But he could double back on us if he wants to. If he does, we'll never see him coming. He'll just swoop down on us and take everything we got."

"That's good to know."

"We got to be careful," Johnny said. "We've got his old lady. I can bet you he's missing that stuff something awful."

"To tell you the truth," Raider replied. "I'm kinda missing it myself, Johnny."

"I think he's gone," Johnny said. "Let's ride back and tell the dan . . . er, Doc about this."

"I wonder why they call him Wounded Wolf?" Raider said, pulling himself into the saddle.

"I ain't sure I know about that," Johnny replied. "I just know one thing—a wounded wolf is the most dangerous critter in God's green country."

"I get your meaning," Raider said. "Let's go find Doc."

They retraced their path to the trail, riding back through the forests until they heard the rattling harnesses of the snail-paced wagon. Doc was puffing on a cheroot, and Little Bright Wing was wearing her usual arrogant pout. Doc reined Judith when Raider and Johnny rode up on them.

"I don't see a deer carcass," Doc said. "No luck, eh?"

"Some," Raider replied. "All of it bad."

"We saw Wounded Wolf," Johnny replied. "He was heading north with a party of braves. There was maybe ten of them."

"Oh, no!" cried Little Bright Wing. "My husband. He's going to get me!"

"Steady, girl," Doc said. "Did he appear to be hostile?"

"No, but he knew we were there," Raider replied. "Johnny thinks he might pay us a surprise visit."

"Then we must by all means take precautions," Doc said.

He coaxed Little Bright Wing into the back of the wagon, where he covered her with a canvas tarp. She didn't mind lying in the bottom of the Studebaker; she was in no hurry to be reunited with her husband.

"I just hope he don't smell her," Johnny said.

"Don't be ridiculous," Doc replied.

"I ain't," Johnny said. "You ain't never knowed an Injun like this one. He's the son of Gray Wolf and the nephew of Chief Joseph."

"And we got something that's his in the bottom of your wagon," Raider rejoined.

"He could be anywhere in these trees," Johnny said. "He moves in the shadows like his brother, the wolf."

"Aren't you being a bit superstitious?" Doc asked.

"Injuns ain't like you and me," Johnny replied. "They got their own laws. They ain't natural."

"I think we better get the hell out of here," cried Little Bright Wing from under the canvas.

"I know a good place to camp," Johnny replied. "And if we make it before nightfall, we might even get another shot at a deer for our supper."

"Lead the way," Doc said.

Johnny started back down the trail, toward the ravine. Doc urged Judith forward, marking the nervous tick in Johnny's neck. The kid was looking back over his shoulder as they moved through the trees. Doc felt a chill down his spine. His own imagination was getting a bit reckless. Suddenly, every shadow in the forest seemed like an Indian.

Raider watched the buck mule deer through the sight of the Sharps, trying to follow the animal as it stepped slowly through the thick trees. The buck wouldn't stop long enough in one spot for Raider to draw a true bead with the cumbersome buffalo rifle; it simply wasn't made for mobility, but rather to be fired from a stationary position.

He reached back and nudged Johnny. Johnny handed Raider his Winchester .30-.30. Raider adjusted the sight and thumbed back the hammer. The shell was already in the chamber. He only had to wait for the buck to present a patch of fur big enough to draw a bead on. The rifle echoed through the forest, buffeting the animal to the ground. Raider and Johnny ran down the wooded incline to where the buck lay bleeding on a bed of leaves.

"You took him good," Johnny said. "Right behind the foreleg. Heart shot. You've been hunting before."

"Once or twice," Raider replied.

Raider bent down and slipped a knife blade into the animal's belly. He made an incision the length of the body, allowing the innards to flow out onto the forest floor. Johnny was already at work on the head, skinning it out, taking the antlers for Raider's trophy. It was a young buck, only four points on the rack. The dark purple meat would be tender after it was roasted over a smoking fire for a few hours.

"I'm getting hungry just thinking about it," Johnny said.

"Doc knows how to make biscuits and gravy, too," Raider replied. "He's got stuff on that wagon that you'd never dream of."

"It's a shame you won't be having meat for supper," said an ominous voice from the woods.

Raider reached for his .44, but the metallic chortle of a rifle lever kept his hands still.

"Don't chance it, big man," said the voice again. "I got the drop on you. That's my buck you got there. I been chasing him through these woods for two hours."

"I just shot this buck, partner," Raider said, his eyes scanning the shadows. "You must have heard the shot just now."

"I heard the shot!" snapped the man in the trees. "But I winged him a couple of miles back. Look on his left haunch."

Raider turned over the carcass. Sure enough, there was a wound on the animal's left hind leg. Raider turned back to the direction of the man's voice. He still could not see him.

"You're right, partner," Raider said. "It's your buck. Come on down and get him. We ain't gonna fight you over one scrawny buck, not with all the game in these woods."

No response from the intruder.

"This buck is ours!" Johnny whispered. "He don't have no right to it. I don't care if he—"

"Hush up," Raider said. "Just do what I do. I want to find out what he really wants. If it's the buck, we got no problems."

Raider started to back away from the kill. As he did, the leaves behind him rustled slightly. Raider spun and caught the movement from the corner of his eye. There seemed to be just one man; he didn't have any accomplices to back him up.

"Come on out and take it," Raider said.

"Ain't never seen a man back off so easy," the voice said. "You wearing something up your sleeve?"

"Nothing," Raider replied. "We just don't want any trouble over something like this. We lost a buck to Wounded Wolf today."

"You saw him too!" the man cried. "Where was he?"

"A half day's ride west of here," Johnny replied. "But he was heading north. When did you see him?"

"'Bout two hours ago," the man replied. "He weren't heading north, though. He was going southeast."

"Damn it!" Johnny said. "He's doubling back."

"Maybe not," Raider said.

"If the boy's right, we could all be in trouble," replied the stranger. "Sure makes that buck seem small now, don't it?"

"Look here," Raider said. "We don't have no truck with you, partner. Why don't you just come on down here and put that rifle away? We'll share the meat, and you can have the skin, since you shot it first."

Silence in the shadows. Raider hoped he wouldn't have to kill the man. It was damned hard to trust strangers, especially in the aftermath of the attack on Johnny. He was risking a lot by trusting a man who had sneaked up on him.

"Y'all don't look like no bushwhackers," the man said. "But I could be wrong. Have been before."

"You're the one who got the drop on us," Johnny said.

"True," the man said with a laugh. "What they call y'all?"

"My name is Raider. I'm a Pinkerton operative. This here's Johnny Welton. We're heading west to the Elk Lodge Valley."

"Welton?" the man called. "You Jack Welton's boy?"

"I am." Johnny said. "And what do they call you?"

"Palmer," the man replied. "I knowed your pa a ways back. He ever say my name to you?"

"Not so's I recall," Johnny said. "But he knowed a lot of people. Friend and foe."

"I'm a friend," the man replied. "Be it the same with you?"

"If you want it to be," Johnny said.

Raider heard a sigh, like the man had made a decision.

"I'm coming down," called the stranger. "My rifle's pointed toward the ground. I'm trusting you not to shoot me."

True to his word, the stunted, grizzled woodsman emerged out of the shadows. Raider could smell the man's buckskins, which were probably a decade old. His face was obscured by a thick, chest-length beard, and a leather hat covered his matted hair. He carried an old Remington carbine, a .43-caliber model that was no longer manufactured. Small eyes that never seemed to focus on anything peered out from under his hat brim.

"Howdy," Raider said. "How long you been out in these woods, partner?"

"Nigh on to a month," Palmer replied. "Been trappping

hereabouts. Got a sod house below the forest. Had a squaw there when I left. Don't know if she's there now, what with old Wounded Wolf sneaking around the whole creation."

"That Injun gives me a scare." Johnny said.

"I'd just as soon not have him around either," Palmer replied.

Palmer looked down at the carcass, examining the spot where Raider had hit the buck. Blood oozed out of the wound, forming a bubble of crimson. The woodsman looked up at Raider.

"Good shot," he said. "Clean kill. To look at you, I'd figure you for a city boy the way you're dressed. I like that fancy hat, cowboy."

"He should see Doc," Johnny replied.

"Doc?"

"A friend," Raider replied.

Palmer glanced at Raider with his glassy eyes.

"Where y'all camped?" Palmer asked.

It would be a sign of trust if they told him the location of their campsite. It would reassure the old trapper that no one was slipping up to conk him from behind. Raider was aware of the rifle barrel, which angled toward the carcass. He could pull on the rifle if he had to, but he sure as hell didn't feel like taking a round at such a short distance.

"Tell him where we're camped, Johnny," Raider said.

"You know the flume?" Johnny replied.

"Up on the crick?" Palmer asked.

"Right," Johnny replied. "We're up on the ledge, above the pool."

"Lots of trout in that pool," Palmer said. "Why'd y'all come after deer?"

"Could ask you the same question," Raider replied.

Palmer tossed the rifle to the ground.

"Hell, mister, I can't stand fish!"

Raider laughed. Palmer went down and went to work on the haunches with a sharp blade. Raider nodded and Johnny continued on the skin.

"Let's get this meat over a fire," Palmer said. "I ain't et since yesterday."

"Looks like we got company for dinner," Johnny said.

Raider just wondered if they could get their guest to take a bath before they ate.

Palmer approved of the campsite. Johnny had found a ledge over a flume, a small gorge with a stream running along a stone bed of rock. A glacier, Doc said, had cut the gorge through the sloping forests in another time. Nobody took much heed of his lecture, however. They were happy just to be camped on a ledge with a wall of solid rock behind them.

Johnny had fashioned a rope ladder for access to the overhang, pulling it up behind them when they were safely on the ledge. Doc built a fire in a circle of stones. Both halves of the dressed-out buck turned on a spit over the fire. Palmer was acting as cook. All of them sat upwind from the pungent trapper.

"Sure is pretty up here," Palmer said, looking straight at Little Bright Wing. "Only seen this place once before."

"We're safe enough up here," Raider said, trying to take Palmer's mind off the woman. "I just wish there was a safer place for the horses."

"Ain't no cause to worry," Palmer said, spitting into the fire. "I'm beholden to you folks for taking me in. I'll stay down with the horses tonight."

"Thank God for that," said Little Bright Wing. "You sure as hell smell like one of them."

Palmer laughed at her.

"She sure is a sassy squaw," Palmer replied. "Who's she belong to?"

"I don't belong to anyone," the girl cried.

"I'll make you a good offer," Palmer said. "She yours, Johnny?"

"She belongs to Wounded Wolf," Doc replied.

Palmer glanced at Doc to read him, to see if he was telling the straight-faced truth.

"Never mind," Palmer said. "Don't want her now."

"I wouldn't sleep with you even to keep warm," said Little Bright Wing.

"Damn me if she ain't sassy," Palmer said, trying to laugh.

Darkness was well upon them by the time the meat was ready. Doc's tin of biscuits had risen in the heat of the stones around the fire. He had also caught juices from the meat for gravy. Palmer thought his methods were "right smart fer a city feller." When dinner was over, they sat in the glow and warmth of the fire, transfixed by the flickering fingers of the flames. Doc shook his head, trying not to lose his sharpness. He wanted to ask their guest several questions.

"Mr. Palmer," Doc said. "Are you aware that Johnny's father was killed by Indians?"

"He wasn't—"

"Quiet, Little Bright Wing," Doc said. "Well, Mr. Palmer?"

"You mean Jack Welton is dead?" Palmer asked.

"He was murdered," Johnny replied.

"Johnny was told that Wounded Wolf killed his pa," Raider said. "You roam these parts pretty much. What did you hear about it, Palmer?"

"Ain't heard nothing," Palmer said. "I sure am sorry to hear your pa is dead, boy. He was a big man in these parts. I didn't know him so good, but I met him and I knowed he was a great one."

"I appreciate that," Johnny said.

"Do you think Wounded Wolf would attack and kill a man like Jack Welton?" Doc asked.

Palmer scratched his matted head.

"I had my trouble with that redskin," Palmer replied.

"What sort of trouble?" Doc asked.

"He caught me once down on the plain," Palmer replied. "I had about fifty pelts, heading for Colorado. He took 'em from me, along with everything else I had. Left me the clothes on my back, but he didn't kill me."

"You just let him take your pelts?" Little Bright Wing asked.

"I never been so damned scared in my life," Palmer said.

"He just came over a hill, like a spirit or something."

"They're pulling your leg," Little Bright Wing replied. "I hate my husband, but I know he didn't kill anybody."

"Now I did hear that the Sioux were having trouble with him," Palmer said. "He wanted to band all Injuns together and start another war. But I heard tell that Chief Gray Wolf's got him under control. That wouldn't mean that you boys have been pulling my leg, would it?"

"Of course not," Doc replied. "You see, Johnny has employed us to find the murderer of his father. We're heading for the Elk Lodge Valley now to pursue the case."

"You the law?" Palmer asked.

"No, we're detectives," Raider replied.

"What's a detective?"

"Someone paid to find things that other people can't," Doc replied. "We try to find the truth, more often than not."

"Think you could find my first wife?" Palmer asked with a grin.

"Probably," Raider replied. "If you gave us a few facts."

"Nah," Palmer rejoined. "She got took off by the Kiowa. I wouldn't want her back after she's been with the Injuns."

"You scab," cried Little Bright Wing. "She'd probably prefer the Kiowa to you!"

"She's sparky," Palmer replied. "I'll give you twenty muskrat pelts for her."

"Not on your life, maggot!" the girl cried.

"Get into your bedroll, girl," Raider said. "I've about had it with your mouth."

She skulked off and climbed in between the two blankets, inching closer to the fire.

"I'm wondering," Doc said to Palmer, "what you're doing in this particular neck of the woods, my friend."

"I told you, I been trapping," Palmer replied.

"Where's your camp?" Raider asked.

"Oh, 'bout three miles east of where that buck fell today," Palmer replied. "I got a cache of pelts and a horse stashed there."

"Do you know a man named Sherman Ivery?" Doc asked,

searching Palmer's face for the truth.

"Can't say as I do," he replied. "Don't know many people."

"You ain't worried about getting back to your camp?" Johnny asked. "What about your pelts?"

"They'll be all right unless Wounded Wolf finds them," Palmer said. "And if he does find them, well, I sure as hell don't want to be there when he does."

That made a lot of sense to all of them.

When he opened his eyes, Raider knew that something wasn't right. The fire had dwindled into a smoldering circle of stones on the ledge. He could hear Doc's snores and the heavy sighs from Johnny Welton. Below them, the stream bubbled over the rocks, perpetuating the steady roar that had lulled Raider to sleep the night before. The sky was morning purple overhead, and it was getting brighter every second. What the hell was wrong?

It was the strange warmth against his back. A foreign scent filled his senses suddenly. A slender body shifted against him. When he rolled over, coarse black hair brushed against his face. Had a wolverine crawled into his bedroll? Worse—it was Little Bright Wing. She had climbed in with him while he was asleep.

"What the hell are you doing in here?" Raider whispered.

She stirred, rolling over to face him, putting her hands on his chest. Sliding her fingers inside his shirt, she rubbed the hair between his pectoral muscles. Raider tried to fight the hardness that he woke with every morning. Why the hell did she have to smell so good?

"This can't be," Raider said.

"Let me stay here just another minute, cowboy," Little Bright Wing replied. "I want to stay warm. It's so cold on the damn trail."

"Too dangerous," Raider said, resting his hands on her soft shoulders.

"You can have it," she replied, rubbing her body against his. "I know you want it. I seen you looking at me. You know you do. Put your hands on my tits."

She pulled up her dress, all the way to her armpits, uncovering her smallish breasts. She guided Raider's fingers to her tiny, hardening nipples. He couldn't resist, even though he knew better.

"Kiss me," said Little Bright Wing. "Nobody ever kisses me."

His lips brushed her thick mouth. Her tongue searched the inside of his mouth like a hungry snake. Her hands were all over him, working their way down his knotted stomach to his crotch. She was like a wildcat. Raider knew it was wrong, but it was too far along. He blamed his own weakness.

"I want that big thing inside me," Little Bright Wing whispered in his ear. "All the girls at Reva's talk about how big you are. They say you're the only one who makes Reva tickle inside. I want to see for myself, cowboy."

"Shush," Raider said. "I don't want the others to hear us."

"Fuck me and I'll shut up," she replied.

Raider happily relented as her fingers fumbled with the buttons of his fly. He reached to help her, but she pushed his hand away. She was much more adept than he could have imagined. In a few seconds, she had it out, stroking the rigidity. Without warning, her head disappeared down into the bedroll.

"What are you doing?" Raider asked.

"I'm going to suck it," she replied.

"Be careful," he said. "Don't bite it off."

She was better than Reva, he thought with a certain twinge of guilt. It felt so damned good. Little Bright Wing did things with her lips and tongue that didn't seem possible. Raider held his breath, trying not to make noise. If Doc caught them, he would probably never hear the end of it.

"Get back up here," Raider commanded.

She crawled back up his body, kissing him all the way. Raider reached for the dark patch between her thighs, dipping his fingers into her wetness. She spread her legs, anticipating Raider's lengthy intrusion.

"I want it now, cowboy," she said.

"Hold your horses, woman."

But she wouldn't. She rolled over, throwing her leg around Raider's hip. He outweighed her by a hundred pounds, but he was completely in her control. She spun her little backside around until she was ready to accept him sideways. Raider felt the moistness against the tip of his penis. As she worked him into her, she gasped for breath.

"You're stretching me," she said.

"You want me to pull out?"

"No, but don't move. Let me do everything. I don't want you to hurt me."

He feared that he might split her into halves. She was so small compared to most of the women he had been with; usually he preferred them big. But Little Bright Wing was damned good. She took him in and out, gripping him with her tightness. Raider held back, prolonging his pleasure. Inside the girl, he was transported back to Reva's, back to her scented sheets and loving arms.

"Roll over on your back," the girl whispered. "I want to finish with me on top."

She clung to him as he rolled over. He barely felt the weight of her body on top of him. But he sure as hell felt the motion of her hips, moving up and down like an overworked pump handle. Men had paid for her, and Raider was certain they had gotten their money's worth. They were both sweating in the cool morning air.

"Do it, cowboy," she said. "Do it inside me. I want to feel it."

Raider thought it best to comply. Doc had stopped snoring, which meant he would be awake any minute—if he wasn't already. When he climaxed inside her, Little Bright Wing let out a sharp cry, an involuntary burst of passion. Her buttocks shook under the bedroll as she reached her own release. Raider put his hand over her mouth to keep her from crying out. She bit his fingers until she drew a little blood.

"Damn you," Raider said, rolling her off him.

"Piss on you, cowboy," she replied. "We both got what we wanted, so shut up."

"Hush. You're going to wake the devil."

"Doc and Johnny are probably awake already," she said. "And what do you care anyway?"

Raider sat up and glanced toward his companions. Doc had risen to his feet already and was stretching toward the sky. He didn't cast a glance in Raider's direction. Little Bright Wing got up and stepped gingerly past Doc to warm herself at the remaining embers of the fire. Raider leapt up and quickly buttoned his pants.

"It ain't what you're thinking," he said to Doc.

"I think nothing, Raider," Doc replied.

"Yeah, sure," Raider muttered.

"Ah," Doc said, quickly changing the subject. "It's a wonderful morning, in spite of the pain in my back. Listen. Just listen to the forest. It's so alive."

Raider listened. He heard the brook and the songbirds in the evergreens overhead. The air was so crisp and still that he could hear the slightest rustling of red cardinal wings flapping between the boughs. He could hear everything. Everything... It hit him then. He knew what had bothered him when he had opened his eyes, before Little Bright Wing had distracted him. It was the sound that *wasn't* there that made his adrenaline flow.

"The horses!" Raider cried. "I don't hear the horses. And your damned mule didn't wake me up braying for food at daybreak."

They climbed down the rope ladder to the ground. Johnny was awakened by the sudden clamor and was right behind them. Little Bright Wing hovered fretfully at the ledge and watched them as they hurried along the brook. She was all too fearful of what had happened.

"They're gone!" Johnny said. "I don't believe it."

"That son of a bitch Palmer stole our mounts," Raider said. "He even took your damned mule."

"Judith!" Doc cried.

"Why'd we ever trust that crusty bastard?" Raider said.

"Don't speak ill of the dead," Johnny replied. "Look over yonder, Raider."

Palmer had been pinned to a fir tree with an Indian war

lance. His throat was sliced from ear to ear, giving him a second, eerie smile beneath his sagging chin. Insects were trapped in the thick, dried blood on his chest. His matted scalp was gone.

"They got him before he could get off a shot," Johnny said.

"Wounded Wolf?" Doc asked.

"That's a Sioux war lance," Johnny replied.

"Damn," Raider said. "I shouldn't have been so quick to bad-mouth Palmer."

"You didn't know," Doc replied. "We should bury him straight away."

"Shame we ain't got a preacher," Johnny said.

"I know a few verses of Scripture," Doc replied. "And I have a small spade in the wagon. Oh, no! The wagon!"

They rushed through the trees to where the Studebaker sat unharmed on the trail. The Indians hadn't touched it. Raider scratched his head.

"Odd," Doc said. "Undisturbed."

"They just didn't want to bother," Johnny said. "It was too much trouble to go through it in the dark."

"Damn them," Doc said. "Damn them all for stealing my Judith."

"It does seem strange that they'd steal a mule," Johnny said. "Indians don't care too much about mules. Unless . . ."

"Unless what?" Doc asked nervously.

"You sure you want to know?" Johnny replied.

"Tell me quickly."

"Well," Johnny replied. "Once in a while the Sioux like to eat one. They like the taste—"

"Enough," Doc cried. "Stop that this instant!"

"We'd better get up there and put old Palmer in the ground," Raider said.

"What do we do after we bury him?" Johnny asked.

"We'll have to walk," Raider said. "Hoof it."

"How will we pull Doc's wagon?" Johnny asked.

"You forget what Palmer told us last night," Raider said. "He has a cache about three miles east of here. Any ideas where that might be?"

"Could be over by Devil's Head," Johnny replied.

"There's three rocks—big boulders marking a spring. That's where I'd put a cache in these parts. But what if Wounded Wolf found it?"

"Then I lose my wagon, too," Doc interjected. "I suggest you get out of here posthaste, Johnny."

"Go on," Raider said. "Take my Winchester."

"You all right, Mr. Weatherbee?" Johnny asked.

It was the first time Johnny had seen Doc lose his composure.

"Just get gone," Raider said. "Don't worry nothing about him. He's just frettin' over his mule."

"I'll hurry," Johnny replied. "If he's got pelts stashed there, I'll bring them, too. We can trade them for horses later. Even get Doc here a new mule."

"Will you get the hell out of here!" Doc cried.

Johnny ran away as fast as he could.

"You don't have to be so hard on the kid," Raider said. "He's just trying to be good to you."

"How dare they take Judith!" Doc exclaimed.

"I just hope Wounded Wolf didn't find the trapper's horse," Raider offered.

Doc twisted around, looking at Raider with a familiar gleam in his eyes. Something had occurred to him over and beyond his grief for his lost mule. Raider waited for him to speak.

"This changes our outlook on Johnny's predicament," Doc said finally. "Palmer was killed by Wounded Wolf."

"Do we know that for certain?" Raider asked.

"No, but it's a logical assumption," Doc replied. "He got in and out without our hearing him. And there's the war lance."

"Yeah," Raider said. "It's the work of a damned sly Injun. But how does it change our case?"

"Don't you see?" Doc replied. "Wounded Wolf killed a white man. The same thing could have happened to Jack Welton."

"That would mean the girl is lying to protect him," Raider offered. "Course, maybe he just wanted the horses, and killing the trapper was the easiest way to get them."

"It's also possible that the two of them had trouble before," Doc replied. "Palmer said that he'd been robbed previously by Wounded Wolf. Hmm. Interesting."

"If Wounded Wolf was just looking for blood, he would have killed us," Raider said.

"We were safe on the ledge," Doc replied.

"Maybe," Raider said. "But if he had wanted us, he would have waited and ambushed us this morning. No, I think he just wanted the horses."

"If he's so cunning, why didn't he wait around to take his wife back?" Doc asked.

"Maybe he just ain't seen her," Raider replied. "We've been hiding her pretty good."

"Yes, in your bedroll," Doc said. "And, of course, now that she's been with you, he might not want her back at all."

"I'd slug you if I didn't know you were grieving over your mule," Raider replied. "Come on, let's get old Palmer underground. The buzzards'll be flying in a couple of hours."

It took them an hour to find a clear spot and dig the shallow grave. They dragged the body to the hole and laid it to rest. Little Bright Wing picked wildflowers and scattered them around the grave. While Raider shoveled the loose dirt over the corpse, Doc recited a few lines of Scripture. Little Bright Wing tore a piece of her dress and wrapped two twigs together in a crude cross shape. Raider finally pulled a log over the grave to keep out scavengers.

"It doesn't come to much," Doc said.

"What?" Raider asked.

"Life," Doc replied.

"You mean death," Raider said.

"Yes, I suppose I do."

Raider could see that he was shattered by the loss of that mangy mule.

"Look," said Little Bright Wing. "Thank God! Thank God!"

Johnny Welton was coming straight toward them, shouting at the top of his lungs, bolting headlong on a gray mare through the morning forest.

CHAPTER SIX

The rains came at them again, drenching the forests, reducing the trail to one muddy impediment after another, playing hell on Doc's wagon. Raider and Johnny were standing knee-deep in a murky puddle, trying to lift the back wheel of the Studebaker over a rock at the bottom of the mire. Doc gently prodded the mare, unable to whip the poor animal in light of Judith's memory. The wagon didn't want to move.

"Little Bright Wing," Doc said. "Take the reins. I'm going to help them push."

"Hurry it up," she replied. "I hate this rain."

"As if I love it!" Doc snapped.

With no regard for his fine attire, Doc leapt off the wagon into the lake-sized puddle, joining Raider and Johnny at the back of the Studebaker. They put their shoulders into the effort, finally raising the back wheel over the rock. They jumped onto the wagon and started forward again, only to find another impasse twenty yards down the road.

"Son-of-a-bitchin' rain," Raider muttered. "I feel like we're back in Oregon."

"Take the reins again," Doc said to the girl.

"Satan take you, dandy," Little Bright Wing replied. "I'm getting off this wagon, I can tell you. I have to go into the bushes right now."

"You can wait," Raider snarled.

"Piss on you if I do," she snapped, jumping from the wagon seat into the undergrowth.

She disappeared in an instant.

"Shit," Raider growled. "She could be in there for an hour. You know how women can be."

"If the gods are with us, she won't return," Doc rejoined.

"I'm wondering now why we took this case," Raider mumbled.

"Leastways the rain is slackening," Johnny said. "The storm'll be over soon. And the roads won't get no worse."

"That's the first note of optimism I've heard from you," Doc replied.

"Look, Doc," Johnny said. "I'm beholden to you and Raider for taking my case. I'm thinking that if anybody can find the truth, it's you two."

Doc only grunted in reply to the compliment.

"I just wanted to say it," Johnny said.

"Tell us again when we're dry and warm," Raider replied. "We might even appreciate it then."

"I just don't want you dropping my case," Johnny said.

"Don't worry, kid," Raider replied. "We never drop a case until we solve it."

He glanced out into the undergrowth.

"Where the devil is that woman?"

An explosion thundered through the trees—a rifle shot, not the clouds overhead. The slug thudded in the water ahead of them. Raider glanced back to his left. A man in a gray slicker was standing at the edge of the trees, aiming a .45-caliber Remington repeater at Raider's head. A dirty bandanna was wrapped around his weathered neck, and a Confederate officer's hat hid most of his grimy face. He moved cautiously toward them, keeping the weapon pointed at Raider, barking his orders as he came.

"Y'all lift your hands," he cried. "I can take you all three before the first un gets off a shot. So don't think about it."

"The storm subsides," Doc muttered. "But now a crusty highwayman waylays us."

"What'd he say?" the man asked.

"Nothing," Raider replied. "It just ain't been our day."

"Things are tough all over," the man said. "Now, listen here. I don't want to kill you. Just throw down whatever you got that's worth a hoot. Do that and we can part friends."

"You're mighty sociable for a thief," Raider said.

"I hear you, mister," the man said, smiling to reveal a mouthful of brown teeth.

He was standing in front of the wagon, brandishing the rifle. He spat a wad of tobacco into the mud and then looked up at Raider. Raider was waiting for the right moment to move for his pistol.

"You talk like a Southerner," the man said to Raider. "You from down my way? From Dixie?"

"Arkansas," Raider replied. "How 'bout you?"

"Louisiana," the man said. "Near the Arkansas border. Hot dang! You and me, we were General Lee's finest."

"I never was able to ride with the general," Raider replied. "But my heart's south of the Mason-Dixon line."

"Rebel scum if you ask me," Doc muttered under his breath.

"Well, I ain't askin' you, now am I?" the man said. "I ought to shoot him for that."

"Don't mind this here Yankee," Raider said. "He's just a little uppity 'cause he thinks his side won the war."

"You 'n' me know better, don't we, Arkansas?" the man replied.

"Name's Raider."

"They call me Cordell Fisk," the man replied.

"You're a long way from home," Raider said.

"Boy howdy, I sure miss Dixie," Fisk replied.

"Well, partner," Raider said, "since we're sons of Dixie, why don't you just get on and let us be."

"Nope, can't do that," Fisk replied. "Got to rob you. I never start nothin' lessen I can finish it. Now, suppose you just toss down whatever you got. I give my word that I won't kill you. Be careful with your gun, Arkansas. I'd hate to spill the blood of a fellow rebel."

There was nothing else to do but look down the barrel of the Remington. Raider looked to be the fastest with a gun, so it made sense that Fisk would shoot him first, Dixie or no Dixie. Then it would be no trouble to kill Doc and Johnny with the next two rounds. At such close range, Fisk wouldn't miss.

"I sure wonder how a loyal supporter of Jefferson Davis can sink so low," Raider said, reaching for the buckle of his gunbelt.

"Watch that gunbelt, Arkansas," Fisk said. "I can nail you to a—"

Little Bright Wing flew out of the trees, landing on Fisk, knocking him into the puddle. A savage war cry erupted from her tiny guts as she clawed his face with her fingernails. Raider dived off the wagon, landing on Fisk's arm, wrestling with him until he had the Remington in hand. Fisk stared down the barrel of his own rifle.

"You can get off him now," Raider said to Little Bright Wing.

Fisk's dirty face had streaks of crimson mixing with the chalky water from the puddle. The girl climbed off and fell back into the mud. Johnny came down to help her.

"She saved our hides," Johnny said.

"And we're thankful," Raider replied. "She can ride next to you in the wagon, Johnny. You can keep her warm."

Fisk climbed slowly to his feet.

"What are you gonna do to me?" he said, looking down the bore of the rifle.

"Johnny," Raider replied, "put the girl on the wagon and then get back up in those trees. Take my rifle. See if this scalawag has a horse tied up anywhere. If you see anybody else, shoot them."

"I'm alone," Fisk said.

"Am I supposed to believe you?" Raider asked.

"Don't take my horse," Fisk begged.

"You was gonna take everything we had," Raider replied.

"As ye may sow, so shall ye reap," Doc rejoined.

"I wasn't gonna kill you," Fisk offered.

"So I won't kill you," Raider replied.

"We're brothers under the rebel flag," Fisk pleaded.

"And for that, I'm not going to turn you over to the law," Raider replied.

"We probably should," Doc said.

"You really want to be bothered by the likes of this?" Raider asked.

"I suppose not," Doc replied. "I leave him to you, Raider."

"Throw me a rope," Raider said to Doc.

Doc pulled the rope off Raider's saddle in the back of the wagon and tossed it to him.

"What are you gonna do to me?" Fisk asked.

"Nothing you wouldn't have done to us, given the chance," Raider replied. "Turn around and put your hands behind you."

"Don't hang me," Fisk pleaded.

Raider tied his hands together and then cut the rope, leaving the rest to throw over a high limb of a pine tree. While Raider formed a slip noose, he leered at the trembling bandit. Fisk's face was white between the streaks of blood and grime. His knees were ready to give way.

"Lie down on the ground," Raider said.

"No, I won't."

Raider pushed him down. Then he looped the noose around Fisk's ankles. Johnny came down through the trees with Fisk's horse just in time to help Raider hoist the bandit up feet first. When Fisk was dangling off the ground, Raider tied the rope to a fir tree. The thief swung in the breeze.

"Hell, Arkansas," Fisk cried. "You gonna leave me upside down like this?"

"Thank your Maker it ain't worse," Raider replied. "Johnny, tie up his horse over there."

"But we need it ourselves," Johnny protested.

"Raider's right," Doc replied. "It's a good wager that the mount is stolen."

"We got enough troubles out here without addin' to them," Raider said. "You want to get hung for having a stolen horse?"

"Yeah, I guess you're right," Johnny said. "But let's at least use the horse to help us get through this stretch of bad road."

"All right," Raider replied. "We'll leave your horse down the trail a piece, Fisk. That is, if you ever get free."

"I'm damned beholden to you," Fisk said with a laugh.

"Damn you, Arkansas. Ain't nobody ever got the best of me till you come along. You sure know how to leave a body hangin'."

Fisk's perverse laughter followed them as the two horses plodded through the trees, heading for the lowlands below the forests.

The trading post at Bishop's Mill rested on the edge of the timberline in a low-lying, depressed flatland that stretched out toward the rolling plains and smaller ranges of mountains. Old men sat on the wooden porch of the rectangular lodge that had been erected from logs dragged down out of the forest by Mose Bishop's late father. The Bishops were surviving their third generation of change in the Montana Territory. Their outpost had been a center for south-central Montana since the first fur trapper came up the Musselshell River.

The trappers had been the true pioneers, Mose Bishop thought. They were hard but not sullen men who simply found that the deserted expanses gave them room to breathe. They fought the Indians and the winters to trade in pelts with Mose's father, who always gave them a fair price. That was when he was a child.

As a young man, Mose had to assume responsibility in a hurry. His father died and left him a business that was changing. The trappers had moved north into Canada. The gold rush brought the miners to replace them. Mose had equipped grubstakers from every imaginable section of the continent, all of them hoping to make good on the glistening flakes of gold in the streams and brooks of the territory. The mother lode was just around the corner, or at least there was enough to trickle down and keep the Bishops well fed.

Now silver was the thing. Most of the silver mining was done by companies, who threw some business to Mose Bishop now and then. His latest customers seemed to be mainly farmers or ranchers. It had been a lot harder to stock the things they needed. Most of them had women along. Mose had taken a ribbing from the old men on his porch about the new bolts of bright cloth that rested on his redwood shelves. They hadn't been so cheerful about the arrival of the barbed wire.

"Times are changing, mister," Bishop said to Raider, who had patiently listened to his story. "Seems like things is closing in on us. Got a ranch not five miles east of here. That's close for these parts. Course, the mines are further north, but there's more cattlemen coming in every day."

"I seen it too," Johnny replied. "The territory's a lot different now."

He was sitting next to the potbellied stove with a blanket wrapped around his shoulders. His buckskins were drying in the heat next to the stove, along with Doc's suit. Doc was outside in the bathhouse behind the trading post. He planned to soak in a hot tub until his clothes were dry. Little Bright Wing was upstairs in the living area with Mose Bishop's squaw. Raider had purchased a pair of trousers, dry socks, and a thick wool shirt from Bishop's shelves. He didn't want to wait around naked while his old clothes dried out.

"When I was a boy, this territory—" Johnny started.

"You was never a boy," Raider interrupted, catching Johnny's fretful eyes.

Raider shook his head, telling Johnny not to volunteer any information about their party. He didn't want word of their arrival to reach the Bar W before they even got there. Doc's artful disguises and schemes would be ineffective if everyone knew that Johnny was bringing the Pinkertons back with him.

"You from these parts, son?" Bishop asked Johnny. "I think maybe I seen you through here before."

"He's from south of here," Raider offered. "Down Colorado way. We just come up here to do some hunting."

"Where'd you pick up the squaw?" Bishop asked.

"Her and the boy are going to be married," Raider replied.

"What?" Johnny said. "I ain't never—"

"I think your buckskins are dry, boy," Raider replied, cutting him off. "Why don't you put them on back in the storeroom?"

"Yeah," Johnny said. "Why don't I?"

Johnny plucked his buckskins off the pegs where they hung on the wall next to the stove. Raider didn't like taking him down a notch in front of the storekeeper, but it had to be done. A youthful mouth could spill a lot of information that might sink them later. Johnny muttered to himself as he disappeared into the back room.

"He's might jumpy, what with the weddin' and all," Raider said. "You wouldn't know it to look at him, but he's crazy about that little girl upstairs."

"I've been happy with my squaw woman," Bishop replied. "She's Kiowa. Traded a grubstake for her back in the gold rush. She gets on me once in a while, but mostly she don't say nothing. Works damned hard, too. And she keeps me warm at night, if you know what I mean?"

Raider laughed.

"I wouldn't mind having me a squaw myself," he said to ingratiate himself with his host. "You got another cup of hot coffee for me, Mr. Bishop?"

"Help yourself," Bishop replied. "It's on the stove over yonder. No charge, either, since you bought them clothes."

Raider poured himself a cup of steaming black coffee. Johnny came back into the room in shrunken buckskins. The rain had left them a size smaller, but they still seemed to fit him.

When Johnny was next to the stove, Raider turned his back to Bishop and whispered to the kid, "From here on out, be careful what you say."

"Yeah, I thought about that when I was gettin' dressed," he replied. "Sorry I almost let my mouth run away with me. Good thing Bishop's got a bad memory. I must've been through here five or six times."

"Yeah, that's part of our luck used up, though," Raider replied. "Go out to the wagon and get the pelts you brought back from Palmer's cache. I'll see if I can get old Bishop there to strike a bargain."

Johnny hurried out to retrieve the furs. Raider turned back to Bishop, who seemed to have missed their private conversation. He was gliding between his overstocked shelves, shifting merchandise from one shelf to another. Raider gave him a second to come around to his side of the counter again.

"You ever hear of a man named Palmer?" Raider asked.

"Yeah," Bishop replied. "I knowed him. Trapper. Not many trappers left in these parts. He was damned mad when I quit stocking traps. He's got a sod house about twelve miles south of here. Keeps a squaw there, I believe."

"He's dead," Raider replied.

"No! Don't that beat all."

"He joined us two days ago," Raider said. "Wounded Wolf cut his throat while the rest of us were sleeping."

"I heared that Injun was hereabouts," Bishop said. "Hope I don't have no trouble with him. How'd you escape him, mister?"

Raider explained how they had slept on the ledge while Palmer had stayed down with the horses. Bishop listened intently, like a man who was used to taking in news of the territory. Just as Raider was finishing the story, Johnny came back in carrying the furs.

"This here is Palmer's cache," Raider said.

"How'd you come by it?" Bishop asked.

"Palmer told us where it was before he was killed," Johnny said. "To show us he trusted us."

Bishop looked at the pelts and then raised an eyebrow at Raider and Johnny.

"How am I s'posed to know you didn't kill him for it?" Bishop asked warily.

"Because I'm tellin' you we didn't," Raider replied. "And if there's a territorial marshal around, you can send for him and I'll give him the truth. We got nothing to hide."

"You know it was Wounded Wolf?" Bishop asked.

"We saw him the same day," Raider replied. "And there's a Sioux war lance in the back of the wagon if you want to look."

"No. No need for that. I believe you," Bishop said.

Johnny tossed the pelts on the counter in front of Bishop.

"There's five mink, three fox, and six marten," Johnny said.

"You want me to trade for them?" Bishop asked.

"What's the matter?" Raider asked.

"Well, Palmer was nearabouts the last trapper left in these parts," Bishop replied. "He never brought his furs to me. He usually took them down to—"

"Mr. Bishop," Raider interrupted. "Don't run me around the bush on this thing. A man's dead, and I ain't about to bargain with his last worldly possessions. Now, I've got his horse, and I aim to keep it. But I want you to take these furs and get what you can for them, understand? Take the money and see that it gets to Palmer's squaw right away."

"Course, I might have to keep something for my trouble," Bishop said.

"Yeah, and you're gonna give me a good price on a pair of horses, too," Raider replied.

"That can be arranged," Bishop said.

Bishop's wife came in through the back room. She went to the stove and checked Doc's clothes, which were now dry.

"Maybe a mule," Johnny said, thinking of Doc's loss.

The squaw headed back to the bathhouse with Doc's suit.

"Don't got no mules," Bishop replied. "But I think I can give you two mounts for a fair price."

"We'll stretch our legs while you work it out," Raider said. "Come on, boy."

Raider started for the door. Johnny fell in beside him, smiling at Raider's tactics.

"And I thought Doc was the smart one," Johnny whispered.

"Neither one of us likes to fool around, boy," Raider replied.

They emerged onto the porch, where the old men sat under an awning that had been made from sapling-thick logs laid between two tree trunks. A mixture of clay and straw had been packed over the logs to keep the rain and snow from leaking between them. Raider and Johnny leaned back against the wall, listening to the improbable tale told by a grizzled old woodsman. Doc soon joined them, looking as if he had just stepped out of Mrs. Paxton's shop. The three of them were hanging on the old coot's words when he stopped and stood up. He peered out toward the rolling afternoon shadows of the plain.

"What are you looking at, old-timer?" Raider asked.

"Man coming," replied the elderly woodsman. "Horse. Coming fast. You can hear him if you listen."

Raider couldn't hear a thing. He glanced at Doc, who also seemed to be in the dark. They gazed out in the same direction as the old man but saw nothing.

"He's right," Johnny said suddenly. "I can hear him now. There. Over that rise."

The rider came up and down a hill like a flea on the ridge of a scratching dog's back. As he got closer, they could hear him yelling at the top of his lungs. He was shouting something about Indians, near as Raider could hear. The horse was almost on them before the rider pulled back the reins. His mount, a chestnut stallion, slid to a halt in the half-dried mud.

"Water," the rider said. "Water. Please."

One of the old men handed him a dipper. Bishop came out of the store to investigate the commotion. The old men were leaning forward with expectant faces. Raider watched the man as he drank from the dipper. He wore a tattered blue cavalry uniform that had been worn by enlisted men of the western armies. He was short, ugly, about forty-five years old, with a fat face and graying hair. An ancient Navy Colt was strapped to his side. It looked like a .36 caliber, Raider thought. The man spat out a mouthful of water and drew his blue sleeve over his lips.

"Injuns," the rider said. "North of here. Attacked the Dandridge place. Killed every one of them sodbusters and burned them out. Took all they owned."

The man went on in hideous detail, describing the positions in which he had found the scalpless bodies—women and children, too. Doc and Raider watched him closely. He was performing the story, having too much fun with it. Doc glanced at Raider, who shrugged his shoulders.

"Think he's lying?" Doc asked in a whisper.

"Maybe," Raider replied. "Why don't you pin him down?"

Doc turned to the man, who was catching his breath again.

"Excuse me, sir," Doc said. "How many Indians were there in the attack?"

"Tracks showed fifteen or twenty," the man replied without hesitation.

"Did you find any mule tracks?" Doc asked.

"Hell, mister," the man replied. "Ain't no difference in horse and mule tracks."

"This would have been different," Doc said. "The mule would have been shod with a special shoe that leaves a four-leaf clover in the track."

"Didn't rightly see that," the man said. "But I'm tellin' you, they had them sodbusters strung up like . . ."

As he went on, Raider noticed that Johnny was standing on the edge of the porch, staring at the rider's mount. Raider moved up behind him, speaking in a low tone so the rider wouldn't hear him.

"What you on to, boy?" he asked.

"That stallion," Johnny said. "The one the man rode in on. It belonged to my father, Raider. That's my pa's horse."

"You sure?" Raider asked.

"Yes," Johnny replied. "I fed that critter every day for five years."

"Check the brand," Raider said.

"That'll be easy," Jonny replied. "Pa always branded his horses where the saddle blanket would cover it up. He thought it was a good way of catching somebody who took your horse."

"Doc's got him busy," Raider said. "Go to it, boy."

"Blood," the man cried as Johnny stepped down off the porch. "Blood was everywhere, so thick it was caked in the dirt. Yes siree. That Wounded Wolf sure did a job on them."

"Wounded Wolf?" Doc said. "How can you be sure it was Wounded Wolf who attacked them?"

"Had to be him," the man replied. "He's the only Injun been causing trouble in these parts. Had three raids this month alone."

Raider was watching Johnny, who lifted up the saddle

blanket on the chestnut stallion. He took a look and jumped back onto the porch next to Raider. It was the Bar W brand all right, he told Raider. Raider nodded and turned his attention back to Doc.

"When did this latest attack occur?" Doc asked.

"Yesterday, near as I could tell," the man replied. "I spotted some Injuns heading north just before daybreak myself. I didn't think nothin' of it until the sodbusters turned up dead."

"And how far from here would you say the sodbusters lived?" Doc asked.

"Day's ride north," the man replied. "I been ridin' this way to warn everyone."

"That probably won't be necessary," Doc replied. "Wounded Wolf did not attack the settlement you're talking about."

The man glared at Doc, who locked eyes with him.

"You callin' me a liar, mister?" the man said, taking a step backward.

"No," Doc replied. "I don't doubt that some sort of attack took place against a settlement near here."

"But you say it weren't Wounded Wolf?" Mose Bishop asked.

"Yesterday morning Wounded Wolf attacked a man in our party named Palmer," Doc replied. "He killed the man and stole our horses while we slept on the ledge above. We were camped a day's ride south of here. I doubt that even Wounded Wolf could cover two day's worth of ground in one day, much less be in two places at the same time."

"It weren't Wounded Wolf who stole your horses," the man protested. "You're lying, dandy."

"There's a Sioux war lance in the back of my wagon to prove I'm not," Doc replied. "Now, suppose you tell us who really attacked that settlement north of here. Or aren't you so eager to tell the truth?"

The man stepped back again, lowering his hand toward the Navy Colt. Raider marked his hand movement. If the man pulled on them, Raider would be ready with his .44.

"Who are you to call me a liar, mister?" the man asked.

"I might ask you the same question," Doc replied.

"Since we're asking questions," Raider chimed in, "how about telling us where you got that horse you're riding, partner?"

The man's brown eyes narrowed. He hadn't expected such a cool reception upon his entrance. Clearly, Doc and Raider had caught him in more than one lie. He moved toward the chestnut with his hand by the butt of his pistol. Johnny jumped between him and the horse.

"Tell the boy to move," the man growled.

"This horse belonged to my pa before he was killed," Johnny said. "Where'd you get it?"

"I bought it in Denver," the man replied.

"If that's the truth, then you have nothing to worry about," Doc said.

"I ain't worried," the man said. "Just git the boy out of my way before someone gets hurt."

"Not until you come clean," Raider replied. "We got a few more questions to ask you. You ever heard of a man named Sherman Ivery?"

"No!" the man snapped. "Now let me be. I got to spread the word about Wounded Wolf."

"Yes, you seem awfully eager to make him famous in these parts," Doc said. "And I think I know why."

The man tried to jump onto his horse, but Johnny pushed him down. The man scrambled to his feet, standing ready with his hand over his holster. Raider lowered his hand as well.

"Don't try it, mister," Raider said. "We don't want to hurt you. . . ."

The man didn't give Raider a chance. His hand fell toward the Navy Colt. Raider beat him to the draw by half a second. The .44 belched fire and lead into the man's chest, while the Navy Colt went off in the air. The man fell backward, blood oozing from the hole in his blue jacket just over his heart. He lay on the ground, twitching as the last current of life flowed out of him. The old men and Mose Bishop were gaping. Doc and Johnny were just as stunned by the untimely showdown. It had happened so fast.

"I didn't want to do that," Raider said.

"He drew first, mister," replied Mose Bishop. "Ain't that right, boys? The stranger pulled on the big man here."

The old men agreed readily.

"He was riding a stolen horse, too," Johnny said.

"He wouldn't have wanted to run if he hadn't been hiding something," Bishop rejoined. "I can't for the life of me figure out what he was hiding."

Doc was sure he had an idea.

"Can you write, Mr. Bishop?" Doc asked.

"Yes, sir, I sure can," Bishop replied.

"Very good," Doc replied. "I want you to write down what you saw here and sign it. Tell exactly what happened. Don't leave anything out. These men can write their own statements, too. Anyone who can't write may sign your statement with his mark. Make sure you get the man's name beneath his mark."

Bishop and the old men eagerly rose to the task, feeling that an official statement somehow made them more important for witnessing the violence. Procedure warranted an official statement anyway, Doc thought. And if any trouble happened with the territorial authorities, they always had the statement as proof of Raider's innocence.

"Why the hell did he draw on you?" Johnny asked Raider.

"We'll discuss it on the trail," Doc replied.

"But I don't understand. . . ."

"Doc's right," Raider replied. "As soon as Bishop's through here, I think we better get the girl and some fresh supplies and get the hell out of here."

"How much farther to the Bar W?" Doc asked.

"Two days, maybe," Johnny replied.

Two days. That wasn't much more, Raider thought, not after all the ground they had covered. He just wondered how many more bodies they would have to scatter along the way.

Three sets of well-shod hooves trodded the spongy turf of the rolling, buffalo-grass plain. Bishop had given Raider a black gelding after he had found the dead man was worth two hundred dollars in reward money. The man's name was Zeb Colter, a former Indian fighter turned convicted horse thief. He had escaped from the territorial prison in New Mexico and was reported heading north to rejoin his old gang in Colorado. The leader of the gang was a man named Bronc Talbot. No other information was listed on the crumpled wanted poster that Bishop dragged out of his desk.

Raider was glad to have a horse under him after bouncing in Doc's wagon on the pothole-filled trail. Johnny was riding proud and sad at the same time on his father's stallion. Little Bright Wing hid under a tarp in the back of the Studebaker, fearing a random clash with her Sioux husband. Raider kept watching Doc, knowing that any minute he would start running off at the mouth. He could see the mill turning behind Doc's eyes.

"We've stumbled onto more luck than we could have hoped for," Doc said. "Luck cannot be counted on, but when it comes, it's worth hours of investigation."

"What have you figured?" Raider asked.

"A gang," Doc said. "Colter was linked to a gang. He was a former Indian fighter. Perhaps he was part of a regiment or a squad that saw action and was eventually reported dead or missing. The men continue to follow their commanding officer because none of them have anyplace else to go. And since they are thought to be dead, the army forgets about them, leaving them to operate as . . . jayhawkers, I believe they're called."

"How'd you think up all that?" Johnny asked.

"Colter was wearing an old army uniform," Doc replied. "So was the man who took a shot at you in San Francisco."

"That's right," Johnny said.

"How does the gang theory sound to you?" Doc asked Raider.

"It's pretty firm ground," Raider replied. "There were gangs of stragglers in the Confederacy after the big war. Johnny here says Ivery brought in guns to help him hold the ranch. If he's got a man named Talbot working for him, we'll know you're right."

"The attack on the settlement to the north vindicates

Wounded Wolf," Doc replied. "If Palmer's murder can be excused."

"So who attacked the sodbusters?" Johnny asked.

"More than likely," Doc replied, "a gang of men masquerading as Indians. In the wake of Wounded Wolf's hunting party and his search for Little Bright Wing—"

"I heard that, dandy," cried the girl under the tarp.

"—the gang pillages at will, blaming the Indians and also lending credence to the story that your father was killed by Wounded Wolf," Doc went on. "It fits together too well to be coincidental."

"You may have it nailed, Doc," Raider said.

"And," Doc continued, "if Little Bright Wing is telling the truth about your father being killed by a lone assassin—"

"And I am," came the muffled reply from the girl.

"—then your father really was shot from a distance and the body was hidden in a place where it would not easily be found," Doc concluded. "Although, I wonder why he was killed in such a cowardly way?"

"Nobody wanted to face Pa head on," Johnny replied. "He was too mean. They'd have to take him at a distance if they were going to . . . If that son of a bitch Colter had anything to do with my pa's death, then I'm glad you plugged him, Raider. The man on the roof, too."

Raider didn't thank him for the compliment. He was thinking about the poor sodbusters who had died in the attack on their farm. Somebody didn't care how many lives it took to cover his tracks. If Colter had been responsible for the deaths of honest people who were just trying to live off the land, then Raider was glad he had killed him too.

"One thing I don't understand," Johnny said. "Why did Colter pull on Raider? Seems like he would have tried to be more sociable. You know, tried to fool us on who he was."

"He might have if we hadn't called him on the stolen horse," Raider replied. "We flushed him, like a mountain lion. He figured we were the law, or close to it. A jayhawker knows when he's got to cut and run."

"I'm guessing that your father's body was taken away

by the gang," Doc said. "They're undoubtedly allied with Ivery."

"And they'll be back at the ranch," Johnny said, "waiting for us. I hope y'all aren't gonna face them all by yourselves."

"You think we're stupid, boy?" Raider replied. "We never do nothin' without a plan. Ol' Doc there will come up with something. And what he don't come up with, I fill in. Get it?"

"What're you gonna do?" Johnny asked.

"We'll have to assess the situation," Doc replied. "We have a good base to work from. We know who we'll be dealing with, but the circumstances require thinking under pressure."

"How much longer till the Elk Lodge Valley?" Raider asked.

"We should see it by tomorrow afternoon," Johnny replied. Earlier if you want to travel through the night."

"I'm agreeable," Doc replied. "Raider?"

"I can sleep in the saddle," Raider said.

"Then on through the cloak of inky night," Doc said with a strangely energetic tune in his voice.

Raider knew that Doc was ready for the investigation. The closer they got to doing their work, the happier Doc became. He didn't even mind riding through the night. And after all they had been through, Raider would have done anything to finally reach the end of a long trail.

CHAPTER SEVEN

The pink bitterroot flowers spread as far as the eye could see in the rolling, bumpy grasslands of the Elk Lodge Valley. Western meadowlarks sailed nonchalantly over the deep green grazing plain, barely missing the blossoms of sweet clover and flowering cactus, gliding between the clumps of cattle that fed in the afternoon sun.

The view was a fitting reward for the journey's end, Raider thought. He stood next to Doc on the narrow plateau that Johnny had referred to as the east ridge. The rise actually marked the southwestern boundary of the Bar W spread, as Johnny had said. To the north lay the low, vague peaks of the Little Belt Mountains. The peaks of Big Snowy lay farther east, barely discernible in the diffused yellow glow of the plain. A late summer chill was in the air, hinting at the threat of an early fall.

"'O'er the smooth enameled green,'" Doc said, gazing out into the vista. "Ever hear of Milton, Raider? *Paradise Lost?*"

"You didn't do this valley justice when you described it," Raider said to Johnny, ignoring Doc's literary reference.

"It's my home," Johnny replied. "And I aim to get it back from Ivery and his sister. They can't keep it from me, Raider. I'll kill them all if I have to."

"Steady, boy," Raider said. "Don't get all worked up and lose your head. We're gonna need you when we go to work."

"I suggest we make camp," Doc interjected. "We can start fresh tomorrow. Do you think my wagon will be safe below, Johnny?"

"We hid it pretty good in those rocks," Johnny replied. "I don't think they'll find it."

They had approached the valley by a circuitous route to avoid a clash with Ivery's men. The ridge was accessible only from a narrow trail that went up one side and down the other. Below them was a stand of boulders that marked the southern pass that was the only entrance to the valley from their direction. No sentries guarded the pass, an indication of Ivery's confidence about his grip on things, Doc thought.

"We'll have to do without a fire," Doc said. "The flame and smoke would surely give us away."

"I get to freeze my ass off again," said Little Bright Wing. "I can tell you I thought I'd never come back to this godforsaken place. I hate this valley."

"Shut your hole," Raider scowled. "Git over there and spread out the bedrolls. And break out some dried meat."

"Want me to put your bedroll next to mine, cowboy?" she asked.

When Raider did not respond, Little Bright Wing went about setting up the bedrolls, clearing the rocks and pebbles, the whole while sticking out her lower lip in a pout.

"Johnny," said Doc. "Come here if you will."

Johnny stepped over next to Doc.

"Explain the layout of the Bar W for me," Doc requested.

"Well, you can see the mountains for yourself," Johnny said. "This ridge is the beginning of the Little Belt foothills."

"But where is the lodge?" Doc asked.

"See that black square, between the hills?" Johnny replied. "That's the roof."

The lodge had been constructed from logs brought in by wagon from the western forests. Johnny's father had set the dwelling in a natural depression between the crests of three rising hills. The roof and smoking chimney were barely visible from the ridge. Jack Welton had put the house in the small valley to form a natural fortress against Indians. From the three rises, a small band of men would enjoy an advantage over any attackers.

"Clever," Doc said. "What about those corrals to the left here? Barbed wire, aren't they?"

"That's Ivery's doin'," Johnny replied. "My pa never liked barbed wire. Ivery built them for holding pens, for the herd. Huh. I don't understand it."

"What?" Doc asked.

"Those pens should be full," Johnny said. "It's gettin' late in the season. Ivery ain't even started the roundup yet."

"I can see the herd," Raider rejoined, pointing to an area a few miles north of the pen.

"Looks bigger than when I left," Johnny said. "Even from here."

"Probably been rustling a few cows in their Indian raids," Raider replied. "Just put it on the list."

"Our man Ivery is quite a fellow," Doc said.

"He's gonna be dead soon," Johnny replied.

"Easy, Johnny," Doc said. "We don't want to move too quickly. We have a certain element of surprise with us. Let's have a good night's sleep and start fresh in the morning. I daresay things will seem a lot clearer then."

They slept in a tight circle, with the three men taking turns on watches of four-hour intervals. Raider drew the midnight watch, sitting cross-legged on the edge of the ridge, his .30-.30 resting on his lap. A quarter moon illuminated the valley below, rendering an infinite variety of shapes and shadows. Raider tried to suppress the grumbling in his nervous stomach, ascribing the night movements to the vividness of his fearful imagination. He finally decided the noise on the path below him was no fantasy.

Animal sounds, he thought. A wolf or coyote, or even a rabbit foraging in the night for food. When loose rocks and pebbles were dislodged on the path, he wondered if a mule deer had come up the path. But the sounds were too

awkward for a light-footed animal, leaving Raider to con-
clude that a human being was ascending from the valley
toward their campsite.

Raider was on his feet immediately, stalking the crunch
of pebbles beneath leather soles. He moved low to the ground
in the half-light until he heard a rustling noise to his left.
He cranked a round into the chamber of the .30-.30. The
footsteps halted in front of him.

"Move and you'll be breathing through your chest," Raider
said to a shadow a few feet away.

"Don't kill me," said a female voice that didn't belong
to Little Bright Wing. "I wasn't trying to escape. Honestly."

Raider had not expected a frightened woman's voice from
the intruder.

"Step closer," he said. "Real slow-like. Keep your hands
over your head."

The woman came toward him. Raider could see the delicate glow of her fair skin in the moonlight. Her scent was
in the air, sweet and pure. Her hands were trembling as she
held them toward the starry sky.

"Doc, Johnny! Muster out," Raider said. "Lady, you got
some explaining to do."

"I promise you," she insisted, "I wasn't trying to escape."

"Escape?"

"I wasn't, really!"

Doc and Johnny came up beside him.

"Caught her sneaking around here," Raider said.

"Diana!" Johnny cried.

"Johnny! Is it you? Is it really you? Oh, I knew you'd
come. I knew you hadn't gone away. I've walked this ridge
every night since you left. I knew you'd come back here.
I knew it!"

Johnny embraced the weeping girl.

"Doc, Raider, this here's my sister, Diana," Johnny replied.

"Pleased to meet you," Doc said. "Shall we find a more
convenient spot to talk?"

They sat in the moonlight, listening to Diana's story.

"They're keeping a close watch on me," Diana said.

"Sometimes Ivery's sister locks me in my room. I have to slip away at night. I came to the ridge because we used to play here as children. I knew my brother would come back. They'll kill me if I try to leave on my own, Johnny. I know it."

"Don't worry," Johnny replied. "I'm back, sis."

"Oh, Johnny, let's leave. Let's go away and let Ivery have the Bar W. I don't want him to kill us."

"I can't leave," Johnny replied. "I'm going to get the ranch back. And Doc and Raider are going to help me."

"Who are you?" Diana asked Doc.

"We're Pinkerton operatives," Doc replied. "We're here to find out who killed your father and bring the culprit to justice."

"It's too late," Diana said. "Ivery is evil, and so is his sister. They brought all of those men to protect them. There are too many of them. I just want to leave, go east or west, just get away."

"Listen to them, Diana," Johnny said. "They're good men, and they can help us. Give them a chance."

"Diana," said Doc, taking her tender hand. "If you don't object, I'd like to ask you a few questions."

She looked to her brother for guidance. Even in the dim moonlight, Raider could see she was beautiful. Johnny nodded, urging her to answer Doc's inquiries.

"How many men are there at the Bar W?" Doc asked.

"I can't be sure," Diana replied.

"Guess," Raider said gently, with reverence for those teary blue eyes.

"Thirty maybe," Diana said. "Yes, I heard Sherman Ivery grumbling about having to feed so many. I think he said thirty."

"Good," Doc replied. "Now you're thinking."

"Have you seen a man named Talbot?" Raider asked.

"No, I don't think so," Diana replied. "I have to stay in my room most of the time. Velma says it's for my own good."

"What are your impressions of Velma Ivery?" Doc asked.

"I hate her!"

"Has she treated you wrongly?" Doc asked.

"No, I suppose not," Diana replied. "But there's something not right about her. And I hate her for what she did to my father. She used him to get the Bar W. She tries to be nice to me, telling me how much she misses him. But I know. I know what she did. She's the one that killed my father. I know it."

"Now, now," Doc said. "I shouldn't dwell on it, Diana. You're much too strong a girl for that."

"Diana, have you ever seen a man who dresses all in black talking to Sherman Ivery?" Raider asked.

"I don't know," Diana said. "There have been so many men that I've never seen before. And I want to get away from them, Johnny."

"No, Diana," Johnny replied.

"Please," she said. "I can't stand it there any longer. If I had run off on my own, they would have caught me and hurt me. And I don't know if I can keep slipping away at night. They might do something horrible if they catch me."

"Dear girl," Doc said. "So far they haven't done you harm. I suspect they have kept you on as insurance against Johnny trying to take back the ranch by force. I'm not telling you to go back, but if you don't, suspicion will be aroused and our investigation may be over before it's begun."

"We're gonna help you when the time is right," Raider said. "But you got to let us study on it some."

"It's our only chance," Johnny replied. "I don't like sending you back there, Diana, but if Doc thinks it's best, I think you should go."

"Johnny, I'm afraid," Diana said.

"So am I, Diana. So am I."

He put his arm around her shoulder.

"All right," she said. "I'll go back."

"That's the spirit, girl," Doc rejoined. "Now, listen closely to me. In the next few days, Raider and I will be infiltrating the Bar W in disguise. If you see us about, it's very important that you not show recognition. No one must have a clue as to our identities. Make no attempt to contact us unless your life is in immediate danger. You must pretend that everything is as it should be."

"As it should be?" Diana sobbed. "My father's gone. Is that how it should be?"

"Vengeance is mine, sayeth the Lord," Raider said. "You got to trust in Him, Diana."

"I wish I could have your kind of faith," Diana replied, "but I'm not always strong. I don't know if the good Lord can get us out of this."

"Well, if He can't," Doc said. "Then maybe we can."

The next morning, as Doc walked the east ridge with Little Bright Wing, he was aware of a glimmering circle ahead of them on the swaybacked top of the rocky rise. The sun was bouncing off a glass, a telescope possibly, belonging to someone who might be looking for intruders. Doc rested his hand on Little Bright Wing's shoulder, stopping her in the path. So far she hadn't been able to find the exact spot from where she had witnessed the shooting of Jack Welton.

"Do you see the reflection?" Doc asked.

"Yeah, it just disappeared behind those rocks. I've seen it for twenty minutes. Did you just now spot it?"

"No," Doc replied. "Run back to the campsite immediately. Tell Johnny and Raider to delay their descent. I may need them."

As Little Bright Wing carried out his command, Doc reached into his coat, fishing the .38 Diamondback from his pocket. He leaned against a huge boulder, watching the path. The flashes from the lens had disappeared entirely. It was only a few minutes before a well-dressed man in a black suit came down the trail. He was resting a tripod over his shoulder, carrying a surveying instrument, not a telescope. Doc stepped out from behind the rock.

"Good day to you, sir," Doc said, brandishing his shiny revolver. "My name is Weatherbee. Might I inquire as to your business in this area?"

If the man holding the tripod was shaken, he didn't show

it. He put down the instrument and tipped his black derby, bowing with a sweeping gesture. Then he smiled and extended his hand to Doc.

"Mr. Weatherbee," replied the nattily dressed gentleman. "I have been in this territory for nearly ten years, and I have yet to meet another gentleman. You cannot imagine how delighted I am to hear someone who is familiar with the English language."

"Why, thank you," Doc said.

"I do hope that I have not intruded on someone's private property," the man continued. "But I am in this vicinity for the purpose of taking topographical readings for the St. Paul Railroad Company of Missouri. This ridge seemed like the perfect place to find a vantage point."

"Are you surveying the Bar W?" Doc asked.

"You mean the ranch?" said the gentleman. "No, I'm taking readings of the land on the other side of this ridge, to the south. My employer is considering a line that would run directly up into the central regions of Montana."

"Interesting," Doc replied. "There would hardly seem to be much profit in such a move. Can you speculate as to their motives?"

"Hardly speculation," the man said. "They're looking for a direct route to the cattle markets of Colorado and Utah. They seem to feel that cattle will go to market by rail from these territories. The cattle drives will become a thing of the past."

"Tell me," Doc inquired, "have you had any previous dealings with a man named Ivery?"

"No, I can't say that I have," the gentleman replied.

Doc put the pistol in his coat pocket.

"Sorry about the firearm," Doc said. "I've learned that one cannot be too cautious in the wilds of this territory."

"Truer words never were spoken," replied the gentleman. "I arrived here from the East nearly ten years go. I came here from Providence, Rhode Island, to work for the Western Montana Gold Company, never stopping to inquire as to the assets of the concern. I was simply too bullheaded, yearning for a more exciting existence. You can imagine my distress when my employers went bankrupt the first month of my tenure."

"It must have been frightfully tough," Doc said, encouraging the man to offer information in his talkative state.

"I was going to leave immediately," the gentleman said, wiping his forehead, "but I couldn't allow myself to give up. It's not terribly brave to surrender so easily."

"And you've managed to find work as a surveyor all this time?"

"I've had to work seven days a week to survive," he replied. "I've done well enough. Of late, the silver companies have required my talents. And now the railroad. Of course, I've had to learn to do other things to support myself between surveying jobs."

"Adaptability," Doc rejoined. "The watchword of the West."

"Mr. Weatherbee, there appears to be a group of people coming this way. Do you know them?"

"They are my associates," Doc replied.

Raider strode first on the path, followed by Johnny and Little Bright Wing. Doc urged Raider to holster his .44. Then he introduced them to the surveyor.

"It's my very great pleasure to meet you," the gentleman said, shaking their hands. "I am Dalton Prescott of Providence, Rhode Island."

"Hell, Doc," said Little Bright Wing. "He talks just like you. Now we got two dandies."

"Please don't embarrass me by being a rude girl," Doc replied.

"He's dressed in black," Raider said. "You know Sherman Ivery, Mr. Prescott?"

"No, I told your companion here the same thing," Prescott replied. "I wonder if you would mind telling me what line you're involved in, Mr. Raider."

"I don't know if I can tell you that," Raider replied.

"Our business is of a rather delicate nature," Doc rejoined. "We're employed by the Pinkerton National Detective Agency, and we're currently investigating a murder."

"Good heavens!" Prescott said. "Rather exciting, isn't it?"

"It could git real excitin' if you go shootin' off your mouth about us," Raider replied.

"I assure you," Prescott said, "I won't mention your presence to anyone."

"You know," Doc said, "you could aid us immeasurably if you would lend us your equipment."

"I am at your disposal, sir," Prescott replied.

"What you got in mind, Doc?" Raider asked.

"You'll see," Doc replied. "Johnny, you'll have to go down into the area south of the ridge. Raider, it will be necessary for you to climb down into those rocks at the point there."

"I get all the chicken-pluckin' jobs," Raider said.

"Sorry," Doc replied.

"It don't matter," Raider said. "I ain't sure I want to hang around with all of this gentlemanly talkin' goin' on."

"Whatever does he mean by that?" Prescott asked.

"Pay no attention to Raider," Doc replied. "If you know him long enough, you'll learn to make allowances."

"Here," said Little Bright Wing, pointing to a spot on the path. "I watched from here. I saw him get killed down there."

"You're sure?" Doc asked.

"Yes," she replied. "Look. I skinned my knee on this rock when I knelt down. There's my blood on this boulder."

"Very good," Doc said.

Doc waved to Johnny, who sat below on his father's stallion in the area just outside the valley. Jack Welton had ridden out to meet someone, probably because it was easier than having his party come through the pass. The assassin had probably lain in wait in the rocks where Raider waited for Doc's signal. Raider had found a path down into the slope of boulders.

"I'll be ready momentarily," said Prescott, who set up his tripod at Little Bright Wing's vantage point.

Doc was hoping to use geometry to discover the exact place where Jack Welton's murderer had waited with a weapon.

"Where was Welton standing after the other men rode off?" he asked the girl.

"He was closer than Johnny," she replied. "A lot closer. Johnny should come toward us."

Doc took off his derby and waved it over his head, prompting Johnny to come forward at a slow gait.

"Tell me when Johnny is in the place where his father was killed," Doc said.

"He has to go to the left," she replied.

"You're pointing toward the right," said Prescott.

"Then he has to go right," she insisted.

Doc extended his arm and Johnny veered in the proper direction.

"There," the girl cried. "That's it."

Doc waved both arms over his head and Johnny stopped, climbing down off the stallion.

"Good," Doc said. "Now, Mr. Prescott, if you would focus your lens on Johnny's chest."

While Prescott worked, Doc scribbled a triangle on a piece of paper. Little Bright Wing was the top point on the three-cornered shape, Johnny was the bottom. The last point, yet unknown, would be the position of the killer, probably in the rocks where Raider stood.

"Now," said Doc, "Johnny and Raider both agree that the maximum range of a weapon powerful enough to kill from a great distance is five hundred yards. If we use that distance as the last leg of our triangle, it should reveal the asassin's hiding place. Try a reading of thirty-three degrees, Mr. Prescott."

"You obviously have a knowledge of my trade, Mr. Weatherbee," replied Prescott as he fixed his eye to the lens.

"I dabble in a bit of everything," Doc said modestly.

"There," Prescott said. "That's fixed on the setting you wanted. You were right. It's directly in the middle of those rocks."

"May I?"

"Certainly."

Doc gazed through the instrument, using hand signals to direct Raider between the rocks. Raider stepped carefully among the boulders, keeping his eyes focused for something out of the ordinary. For twenty minutes he didn't see a thing.

"Nothing," Doc said. "Try another angle. Thirty degrees."

Prescott reset the instrument. Raider grumbled as he wound through the stone monuments. He came to a flat boulder with scratches on the top. Raider looked all around the base of the rock but came up empty. He used his fingers to reach into a crack between the boulder and another rock, praying the he wouldn't find a bull snake or a rattler. He felt something metallic in the crack.

"He's waving," Doc said. "He's found what we were looking for."

"Good job, Mr. Weatherbee," replied Prescott.

Raider rejoined them on the ridge, followed by Johnny Welton. Raider opened his hand, revealing a large brass cartridge. The killer had shot from the rocks, reloading in case the first bullet didn't get the job done. When he was satisfied that Welton was dead, he had left up the path Raider had discovered. Little Bright Wing had been telling the truth.

"What kind of gun would you say, Johnny?" Raider asked.

"Buffalo rifle," Johnny replied. "Probably a Sharps. This is a fifty-caliber shell. Probably used an overload."

"How utterly horrible!" Prescott exclaimed.

"We still don't have a body," Raider replied.

"Not yet," Doc replied. "But an hour ago we didn't have this cartridge, either. The next step is to find the rifle that this shell was fired from."

"Where do you propose to look?" asked Prescott.

"In the lair of Sherman Ivery," Doc replied.

"It's about time we took a look," Johnny said.

"You're not taking anything," Doc replied.

"But . . ."

"We intend to infiltrate their defenses using disguises," Doc said. "You'd be recognized at once. No, I want you to stay here to protect Little Bright Wing and our friend Mr. Prescott."

"But I am unable to stay," Prescott replied. "I have to return to Helena to report my findings to my employer."

"Who is?" Doc asked.

"I was hired by a man named Barrow, Reginald Barrow," Prescott replied.

"Does he maintain an office in Helena?" Doc asked.

"Yes," Prescott replied. "Do you intend to visit him?"

"Eventually," Doc replied. "But only after we've finished our business here."

"Does that mean we're goin' in?" Raider asked.

"Yes," Doc replied. "I'll employ my usual guise as a traveling apothecary."

"What do I do?" Raider asked.

"I'm afraid you must attempt a most dangerous undertaking," Doc replied.

"Plucking another chicken, huh?" Raider scowled.

"If we're successful, most assuredly," Doc replied.

CHAPTER EIGHT

Doc's wagon slipped through the narrow pass, between the high, shiny, lichen-covered walls that split the ridge in two. The trail through the pass was rocky and winding. As the gray mare labored on the uneven passageway, Doc couldn't help thinking of Judith and how much easier it would have been for her to pull the Studebaker into the Elk Lodge Valley.

The wagon wheels rolled easier on a road of rich, packed earth that stretched deep-black and thick between the giant puzzle pieces of buffalo grass. It was not a real valley, Doc thought, but more like a basin for the higher grounds of the small mountain ranges. The sloping plane of the landscape was just as awe-inspiring from ground level.

Doc half expected to be set upon as soon as he cleared the pass, but no one came to meet him. Were the usurpers of the Bar W really that confident, or just that careless? Careless men often left their fates to a gamble, one roll of the dice for all or nothing. Gamblers usually played until they had nothing left to play with, Doc thought.

The wagon went over a rise and down the other side. Doc saw the ranch house as he came down the slope. There was also another surprise visible in the depression of the plain. A group of ragged men were bivouacked behind the main lodge. They were hidden from the view from up on the ridge. Doc's rattling wheels mustered the men out of the tents. They obviously weren't expecting a visitor.

Doc reined the mare in front of the lodge. The facade of the log dwelling was covered with the skins of animals—moose, bear, elk, deer, and mountain lion—trophies of Jack Welton's past hunting parties. A small man was removing the skins with a hammer, probably at the behest of the new residents, Doc thought.

"Excuse me, sir," Doc said to the man. "Have I reached the Bar W ranch?"

"No, sir," the man replied. "Used to be called that. Now it's the Double I."

"Never mind," Doc said. "I'm happy only to reach my destination. They told me I was crazy for heading this way. But I told them that people everywhere need cures of all kinds. Tell me, sir, are you well acquainted with the laxative qualities of buckthorn bark? Hyssop is good also. Loosens the bowels remarkably."

Doc tossed the man a piece of sugar candy.

"Contains peppermint," Doc said. "Better than coffee for steadying a man's nerves."

"Thanks," the man said, popping the candy into his mouth.

"Perhaps you would be so good as to inform the proprietors of this household that Lazarus B. Weatherbee is here to cure their ills. Hurry, lad, I'd like to ply my trade while there's still enough daylight."

The man disappeared into the lodge. Behind Doc's wagon, the bivouacked men had gathered in a ragged clump, lurking in unison thirty feet away. Doc turned back to toss them a handful of sugar candy, which a few of them plucked from the ground.

"Come closer," Doc said, to show he wasn't afraid of them. "I can sell you tonics that you've never dreamed of."

But none of them were buying, so Doc turned back in time to see the man come out of the lodge.

"You're to pull around to the side of the house," the man said. "That way."

"Thank you, my good man," Doc replied. "Here, have another piece of candy."

Doc wheeled around the right side of the house, coming face to face with the strangest sight he had seen in the territory. A Colonial veranda, complete with white columns and spindled railing, had been erected on the wall. Seated in fine wicker chairs were two men and a woman. Doc spotted the family resemblance in the Ivery's right away. Both were well manicured and impeccably dressed. The third member of their porch party was a rugged, scarred giant of a man—an ogre, Doc thought. The leader of the bivouacked men.

"You say you have potions to sell?" asked the brother.

Doc studied his handsome, pampered face. He wore the gaudy regalia of a dude—fine linen suit, silk shirt, expensive English riding boots. Tasteless attire, Doc thought. His thin fingers lifted a cigarillo to his aristocratic lips. He was younger than his sister and not nearly as menacing as Doc had expected him to be. Doc knew immediately why he needed a gang of men to protect him. Sherman Ivery wasn't going to stand eye to eye with anyone.

"Potions?" Doc replied. "Sir, I'd take offense if I hadn't come so far to help you. I have more than mere potions to offer you. I have the elixirs and tonics of life."

"Do you have any tonics for my hair?" asked Sherman Ivery.

He laughed as if he had told the funniest joke in history. He ran his smooth hands over his wavy black hair. Doc produced his own bottle of French lilac water, tossing it to Ivery, who caught it between his delicate fingers. The woman laughed heartily, as did the ogre.

"Free of charge," Doc said. "If only you'll listen to me for a moment."

"Well, it certainly doesn't cost to listen," said the woman. "Thank the man, Sherman."

"Thank you, Mr. Weatherbee."

"What else have you got to offer us?" asked Velma Ivery Welton.

Doc looked directly into her green eyes for the first time.

She was older than her brother, perhaps by ten years. But she maintained herself well, exuding a bewitching feminine knowledge that came with maturity. Raider would have called her a black-haired witch. To Doc, she was a beautiful sorceress.

"Madam," said Doc, tearing himself away from her devastating irises. "I can offer you the finest ointments and tinctures known to science. I have cures for indigestion, elixirs to boost your spirits, and laxatives to relieve the pressures of life in the frontier territory."

Velma Ivery rose from her chair, perching her rounded backside on the veranda railing. She allowed her shawl to drop, exposing most of her ample bosom. Doc ignored her, playing the gentleman. She was quite attractive, and he had no trouble recognizing the flirtation. He was tempted to flirt himself. Where had she found such potent perfume in the wilds of Montana?

"Could you cure a sore foot?" she asked.

"You don't have a sore foot," her brother rejoined.

"I do," she insisted.

"Probably a stone bruise," Doc replied. "Full of stones, this territory. Are you in much pain?"

"Enough," she said.

"Perhaps you should soak it in hot water with some of my salts. With a gentle massage, the pain will be gone in no time at all."

"I don't know anyone skilled in the art of massage," replied Velma Ivery, the amorous glint in her eyes more and more obvious.

"I'll do it for ye," said the ogre.

Doc thought the brutish face should belong to a bare-knuckles fighter who had never won a single round.

"One more remark like that and you'll be sleeping in a tent again," warned Velma Ivery. "Is that clear, Mr. Talbot?"

"She don't like me," Bronc Talbot said to Doc.

Doc's theory was proven. Ivery had hired a gang of deserters led by Talbot. Now came the problem of proving how they had killed Johnny's father. Doc saw the beginnings of an opportunity in Velma Ivery's green eyes.

"Do you have any mild soaps?" she asked.

"I could mix some bath oils for you," Doc replied. "Or fine salts, as fresh as the ones used in Cleopatra's tub, drawn from the waters of the Nile itself."

"Would you come into the house and assist me with my foot?" she asked.

"I couldn't, madam," Doc replied. "I'm dusty from the trail and I surely—"

"You may use the bathhouse," she said.

"But of course," Doc replied. "I wouldn't think of being received by such a lady without the proper grooming."

"He sure's got a slick tongue," Talbot grunted. "What the hell are you doin' way out here, dandy?"

"Business has been slow," Doc replied. "I decided to try my luck by branching out into the territory."

"You come a long way for nothin'," Talbot replied, spitting on the veranda's planked floor.

"Get that animal out of here right now!" cried Velma Ivery.

"Go on, Bronc," her brother replied. "It's time to start getting the cattle into the pens anyway."

"I ain't no trail boss." Talbot scowled.

"We pay you to do what we tell you," the woman replied. "Now get out of here before I really become angry."

"I told you she don't like me." Talbot chortled, and with an agility surprising in a big man, he hopped over the veranda railing. He straightened his gunbelt, which holstered a shiny, new Colt .45. He glanced back up at the woman with glassy hateful eyes.

" I don't like nobody talking mean to me," Talbot said. "Just keep that in mind."

He lumbered off with his fists clenched by his sides. A dangerous man, Doc thought. Even Raider would have his hands full if he went toe to toe with Bronc Talbot. Doc almost regretted the second half of his plan.

"Why did you have to do that?" Sherman said angrily. "I told you not to make him mad. He might turn on us if we—"

"I thought you handled him quite well," Doc said.

"I have an understanding of men," said Velma Ivery. "Now, about your bath, Mr. Weatherbee."

Raider stared at his own reflection in the bottom of a shiny tin cup, rubbing a streak of dirt across the bridge of his nose to make it look as though the cartilage had been broken once. The ten-day growth of beard and a crumpled felt hat made him as scraggly as the men who were bivouacked at the Bar W. A worn bandanna and an eye patch filled out the disguise. He pulled down the brim of the hat to hide his uncovered eye.

"You look scary," said Little Bright Wing.

"That's the way I'm s'posed to look," Raider replied.

"Well, I can tell you, you really scare the hell out of me," she said.

She meant it as a compliment.

"Thanks," Raider replied.

"I still wish there was something I could do," Johnny moaned.

He was itching for some kind of activity. Doc and Raider knew better than to let him loose. Raider tossed him the five-power telescope that Doc had left behind.

"Stay right here and keep an eye on us," Raider said. "That's important."

"Just wait?" Johnny asked.

"Who's gonna help us out if we get stuck down there?"

"But . . ."

"You, Johnny boy. If one of us ain't back on this ridge by tomorrow night, you run for Helena. Tell the territorial marshal and wire the Pinkerton Agency in Chicago. Get some help and bring it back. Be patient, boy."

"That's what Doc said," Johnny replied. "He can really spout it off. Know what he said to me? 'They also serve who stand and wait.' Told me to remember it."

"He seems to know about them things," Raider replied. "You just keep your eyes peeled to that telescope."

"I'll come in if there's trouble," Johnny said.

"Don't come in even if they're about to string us up,"

Raider warned. "I mean it."

"I don't like runnin'," Johnny replied.

"Better than dyin'," Raider said.

Johnny extended the spyglass and peered toward the ranch house. He could see the top of the roof and the smoke from the chimney. How would he even know if Doc and Raider were in trouble? He could hardly see a thing.

"I wonder if Doc's inside?" Johnny asked.

"I'm gonna give him another hour," Raider replied. "He should know something by then. If he stays, okay, otherwise I meet him on the way out."

"Raider," said Little Bright Wing.

"Yeah, honey?"

"Well, I want to talk to you," she replied.

"So spit it out," Raider said.

"Don't say it like that, Raider," she replied. "I . . . I want you to have this."

She thrust a polished stone into his hands. It had Indian markings on it. Medicine, Raider thought. In her own superstitious way, she was trying to tell him good luck.

"Why'd you give this to me?" he asked.

"I don't know," she replied. "It's just . . . Doc's askin' you to try to join that gang. It's so dangerous."

"Don't worry about me," Raider said.

"But I am worrying," she replied. "I like you, Raider. I really like you. I have feelings. Just because I take money for—"

"Okay," Raider interjected. "I appreciate this good-luck charm. Only, when it's depending on my life, I'll take the good Lord every time."

"Sometimes it's better to be lucky than good," Johnny replied.

"You're startin' to talk like Doc," Raider said. "I better get movin'. Y'all lay low till one of us gets back."

"Kiss me, cowboy," said Little Bright Wing.

She launched her body onto his, wrapping her arms around his shoulders, kissing him all over the face.

"You can have it when you get back," she whispered. "I'll give it to you like you've never had it before."

Raider was flushed as he headed down the trail to his mount below. When he was in the saddle, he became perturbed with the eye patch and threw it away. He wanted two eyes when he rode down on the leader of the gang at the Bar W. And he had a feeling he was going to need both of them.

CHAPTER NINE

The bathhouse at the Bar W had been framed inside and out in tongue-and-groove heart redwood that must have taken months to arrive from California, Doc thought. He allowed himself an extra five minutes in the hot water, trying to soak away the anxieties of being in the midst of the enemy. A bath had to be appreciated when it came along, no matter where one found it.

"More water?" asked the man who had greeted him earlier in the day.

"I believe I could use another bucket," Doc replied.

Doc watched the man, who limped to the wooden stove where the kettles of water steamed over a fire. A long black chimney of stovepipe protruded from the flat iron heater out of the redwood roof. The man poured the last kettle of hot water into the tub. He was small in voice and stature, still a boy despite his age.

"It stays warm in here all winter," he said. "You can take a bath when it's thirty below. Have to dry off before you go outside."

His face was lined and defeated. He never looked Doc directly in the eye. A foolish man, probably the brunt of more than one joke. A servant, loyal only to his work, soft-spoken and timid.

"What's your name, sir?" Doc asked.

"My real name's Harold," he replied. "But everyone calls me Toby around here?"

"How long have you been riding with Talbot, Toby?"

"Oh, I don't ride with him," he said softly. "I hired on here last month. I do handy jobs for Miss Velma."

"Did you ever know Jack Welton?" Doc asked.

"How did you know about him?" Toby cried.

"Shh, please," Doc replied. "Don't say anything else, Toby."

"Are you some kind of law or something?"

"No," Doc replied. "I'm your friend."

"Haven't had many friends," Toby replied. "Mr. Welton was my friend. I liked him."

"Then you did work for him?" Doc asked.

"Yes, sir," Toby replied. "I just didn't want to tell you. I'm ashamed of what happened to him. I'm ashamed that I kept working here after he was killed. But I needed a job."

"There's no need to be ashamed," Doc said.

"I never worked for nobody but Mr. Welton," Toby continued. "It broke my heart when they made Johnny go. But what could I do?"

He was slow-witted, but rather loyal and conscience-stricken; a possible ally, Doc thought.

"Toby," Doc said. "I'm your friend. Say nothing more about Jack Welton or Johnny. And don't worry."

"Who are you, mister?" Toby asked.

"I'm the man with the peppermint candy," Doc replied. "Now, if you'd like another treat, you should bring me my clothes."

"Can't do that," Toby replied. "Miss Ivery gave them to the Mexican girl to clean. She wants you to wear this robe."

He pointed to a thick white robe hanging on a peg in the redwood wall. What did the widow have in mind? Doc gestured for the robe and Toby held it up for him to slip into. The material was the finest spun cotton.

"Your employer has certainly brought her fine tastes to the territory," Doc said. "Do you have my boots?"

"Wear these Indian moccasins," Toby replied. "We have

to go pretty soon. Miss Ivery wants to see you."

"Lead the way, Toby," Doc said. "I'm wondering what Miss Ivery has in store for me. Or is it Mrs. Welton?"

"She don't like to be called that," Toby replied. "No, sir, call her Miss Ivery."

Doc trekked from the bathhouse to the lodge, following in Toby's muddy footprints. He removed the moccasins in the kitchen and stood on the cool wooden floors. The lodge was a bizarre mixture of western utility and eastern opulence—no doubt the collision of the late Jack Welton and his surviving wife.

The lodge had been constructed on a frame of ponderosa pine tree trunks that had been shorn of their bark, smoothed, and allowed to sit in the elements for a period close to a year. Doc had read about the technique in an architectural journal published in San Francisco. Smaller logs were pegged in place to form the walls and roof, sealed with plaster made from clay deposits near a local river. There were high cathedral walls, with living quarters in the loft area over the main parlor. The parlor was split conspicuously in two halves by a pink stucco wall, which had been erected for Velma Ivery with much finer plaster than that from the river.

"There used to be bearskins all over," Toby said. "Buffalo, too. Miss Ivery made me take 'em down. Said they stunk. I didn't think they stunk. I sleep in the barn. I know what stinks."

"How did she do it?" Doc asked. "I'm utterly baffled. The veranda. And now this."

"She's waiting for you," Toby said. "Just go in. That's what she told me to tell you."

"My coat pocket is full of candy, Toby," Doc replied. "Keep your eyes open. I'll see you again."

There was an oak door in the middle of the pink stucco wall. The portal had been carved exquisitely and fitted with fine brass handles. Doc knocked lightly and heard the widow bid him enter. Her chamber was more than a bedroom; it also served as a study. A marble-topped table beside her brass bed was full of documents that had been rolled into neat cylindrical piles. The rest of the small room had been overly furnished, with something crammed into every corner.

"Hello, Mr. Weatherbee," said Doc's sultry hostess.

Velma Ivery was perched on an Italian love seat, her well-turned foot and ankle soaking in a porcelain bowl. Her maroon dressing down was open enough to make Doc look away. She had on the type of garment he had seen the girls at Reva's wearing. Her breasts swung loosely under the robe as she leaned toward him.

"Are you ready to massage my foot?" she asked.

Doc had to stall. He knew what she wanted as she lifted her foot from the bowl and wiggled her toes at him. And he thought to himself that it would be the height of unprofessionalism to let Miss Velma Ivery's exotic fragrance get the better of him. If Raider was on time with his entrance, Doc might have a chance to look through the papers on the marble table.

"I'm simply amazed by the results you've realized here at the ranch," Doc said. "Why, your taste is impeccable. How did you get all these things into this valley?"

"We shipped them up from St. Louis by steamer," she replied proudly. "Freight wagons brought everything to the lodge."

"You've admirable resolve," Doc said.

"I get what I want, Mr. Weatherbee," replied his hostess. "And I want you to massage my foot for me."

"The salts are working, are they not?"

"Are you nervous in my presence, Mr. Weatherbee?" she asked.

"Oh, no, I assure you I'm not," Doc replied. "I just find it odd that a woman of your refinement has chosen to live in this bleak territory. Are you from St. Louis originally?"

"My foot, Mr. Weatherbee," she said. "Before I call my brother and his friend, Mr. Talbot."

"Your brother might not approve—"

"He does what I tell him," she rejoined. "Like all of the men around here. Of course, you don't have to look at my foot. But I'm going to be angry if you let me walk around in pain."

"No, of course not," Doc replied. "I can't let you walk around in pain, can I?"

Doc knelt down and took her dainty foot into his hands. He examined it closely, aware that she had perfumed her ankles. Ten days on the trail, in close proximity to Little Bright Wing, had done immeasurable damage to his ability to resist the comforts of life. Where the deuce was Raider?

"Are you unmarried, then?" Doc asked.

"I'm recently a widow," she replied. "I was married to an animal. A crusty, ill-mannered hunter who wanted to be a cattleman. But I changed him. This parlor is evidence of that. And I earned it too. I had to do things no woman should have to endure. I . . ."

She caught herself before she said too much. Doc looked up at her vacant green eyes. She brought out the smile, Delilah's own countenance. Doc was afraid of her hunger. But if Raider didn't hurry up, he would be unable to avoid it.

"Does your foot feel better?" Doc asked.

"Yes it does," she replied. "You can stop if you like."

"No," Doc said. "I'll just work out the rest of the pain. I don't mind at all. How did you hurt your foot anyway?"

"I tripped as I was walking," she replied. "I took quite a tumble. I bruised my hip, I think. Would you take a look at it for me, Doctor?"

"I couldn't," Doc replied, dropping her foot back into the bowl. "You see, I'm not a real doctor at all. Just an apothecary."

"It won't kill you to look," she replied.

Doc wondered if she might kill him if he *didn't* look.

"Very well," he said reluctantly.

Her green irises flashed devilishly as she lifted her gown above her hip. She shifted on the sofa, turning her ample hips toward Doc. The white skin of her buttocks was smooth and tight. Doc glanced hastily at her unbruised hip and then looked back up into her mischievous irises.

"I believe you'll live," Doc said.

She laughed at him, dropping the gown, leaning forward to caress his face in her pampered hands. She kissed him like a conqueror taking spoils, as if she could celebrate her recent triumph with Doc's manly performance. As her tongue slipped between his lips, Doc was cautiously aware that his manhood was beginning to perform on its own. Damn Raider and his tardiness!

"Please, Miss Ivery," Doc said, breaking away. "You shouldn't exert yourself until your hip has completely healed."

"Do you know how long it's been since I've had a man?"

"Too long, I'd imagine."

"I mean a clean man with tight muscles," she said. "A man who smells like a human being."

"Miss Ivery..."

"I want you, Mr. Weatherbee," she persisted. "You can cure me with something besides medicine."

He was caught in her web. Best to have it over, he reasoned. The female spider often devoured the male after the consummation of the fertility act. Doc felt rather like an arachnid himself. There was still the remote possibility that he might enjoy it.

"Perhaps we would find more room on the bed," Doc offered.

"Yes," hissed the black widow.

She grasped his hand, pulling him toward the goose-down mattress. She hung her robe on the brass frame and then stepped out of her scant undergarment. Her body was full and olive-skinned, like that of a Mediterranean goddess. Large round nipples and a curly black patch of feminity were temptations beyond any man.

"Am I beautiful?" she asked.

"Yes, you are," he replied, knowing she had to hear it.

She tore the robe from his shoulders and ran her fingers down the tight line of his stomach. Her fingertips found him hard and ready. Doc pressed his face into her heaving bosom, kissing the tips of her brown nipples.

"You're so hard," she whispered in his ear. "Let's hurry. I want it inside me."

She glided onto the mattress, stretching out her voluptuous body on burgundy satin sheets. Her thighs were parted, ready to accept Doc's rigid intrusion. He felt himself drawn onto the bed with her. His hips fell between her legs, and she guided him inside with a quick motion.

"Oh, God," she moaned.

Her back arched, and she dug her fingernails into Doc's buttocks. He had been prepared to perform admirably for the sake of their investigation, but he was finally not called upon to do so. Instead his hostess assumed the lead, bucking beneath him like a wild mustang mare in the middle of the mating season. Doc simply held on, gazing down at her contorted face. She took her pleasure from him the way she seemed to take everything else in her world—forcefully.

"Not yet," she moaned, slowing her motion. "Not yet."

She held him inside her, doing unexpected things with the tight muscles in her vagina. Her thick legs were wrapped around his waist, making him a prisoner between her thighs. She grabbed his hair and pulled his face down, invading his mouth with her searching tongue. Doc wondered if she would ever have enough of it.

"I love to feel it in there," she moaned.

"I'd like to have it off myself," Doc replied.

"Don't be selfish," she cooed. "You don't have it in you to make me surrender."

"Perhaps I should be selfish," Doc replied.

He felt the need to assert himself. Letting her take charge had been a mistake that he was determined to correct. He put his hands down on the mattress and raised the top half of his body.

"Let us just see what I have in me," Doc said.

He started a rocking motion with his hips, rattling the bed springs as he drove his cock in and out of her. Her head went back with a gasp. She muttered obscenities beneath her breath, meeting each motion of his hips with her own efforts. She enjoyed his mastery of her without surrendering, crying out in throaty chortles.

"Harder," she cried. "As hard as you can."

Doc thought that the entire household must be aware of their clamor. He closed his eyes and concentrated, trying to put aside the fear and nervousness to attain his own climax. He thought of Mrs. Paxton, her scent much more appealing than the fragrance that now filled his senses. It was Mrs. Paxton who allowed him to achieve his release, but it was Velma Ivery's voluptuous body quivering beneath him with a climactic breathiness.

"A wonderful prescription, Doctor," said Velma Ivery.

When her breathing began to steady, Doc rolled off her. She stared up at the ceiling with a blank gleam in her witch's eyes. Doc had once speculated that she might be innocent in the business of usurping the Bar W. Instead, she was the reigning queen of misrule, in charge of the entire treachery, or so it seemed. Was there a king behind the royal lady?

"I trust you are delighted by my selfishness," Doc said.

"For now," she replied.

Rolling over toward him, Velma Ivery reached between his legs and grabbed the half-erect flesh that lay there. She seemed to have more energy than when they had started. Was she waiting for Doc to become aroused again? The queen was insatiable.

"I find it incredible that you don't have suitors, even in this uncivilized territory," Doc said.

"You're the first man I've slept with since I became a widow," she said. "I don't meet many gentlemen out here. Would you like to stay on for a few days, Mr. Weatherbee? You won't regret it."

"A day or two might not hurt me," Doc replied. "Perhaps I will stay on."

He wanted to get a look at the papers on her private table. They might contain a clue to the dealings that had brought Johnny's rightful inheritance into Velma Ivery's hands. If Doc had to endure the widow's attentions, then he would simply have to bear up.

Her ministrations between his thighs left him to wonder if she would ever leave him alone in her chamber. She was brimming with a need to share her willing body. She liked to talk, too, so if Doc simply listened, he might pick up a piece of incriminating evidence.

"You aren't coming back to life," she said as she jerked on Doc's phallus. "Have you eaten today?"

"No, I haven't," Doc replied, hoping she would leave to fetch a dinner tray.

"I'll ring for Toby," she said.

Then she would not leave him alone. She reached for a servant's bell, but a knocking at the door preceded her command. Doc quickly donned his white robe while Velma Ivery stepped into her dressing gown. Toby came in at her imperial order.

"Ah, Toby," said Miss Ivery. "I was just about to ring for you. You must have been listening at the door."

"No ma'am," Toby replied. "Mr. Sherman sent me. There's some trouble down by the tents."

"Damn that Talbot," she cried. "I knew it was a mistake to hire him and his cutthroats. Are they making trouble again?"

"No, it's another man," Toby replied. "A big man just rode up out of nowhere and says he wants to join the gang."

Raider! Doc thought. Tardy as he was, his entrance was still well timed.

"Thank you, Toby," said Velma Ivery. "I'll see to it. Do you mind if I leave you alone for a moment, Mr. Weatherbee?"

"No, of course not," Doc replied.

Raider had no idea how well he had performed in his part of the plan.

"On second thought," said Velma Ivery, "I can leave Toby with you. Toby, stay here with Mr. Weatherbee and see to his needs. Bring him anything he wants. I want him to be strong when I get back."

She flowed out of the room like a baroness. Doc looked into Toby's bewildered eyes. The man who had given him candy had betrayed him with his former employer's wife. His simple mind saw it that way, Doc thought.

"Toby," Doc said, "would you fetch my clothes for me?"

Toby turned and exited without a word to Doc. As soon as the door was closed, Doc hurried to the marble table, picking up the first rolled parchment. His fingers were fumbling nervously with the ribbon around the paper as Toby came back into the room holding Doc's suit on a hanger.

"What are you doing?" Toby asked.

"I'm trying to help Johnny and Diana," Doc replied.

"The way you talked in the bathhouse, I thought you were a friend to Mr. Welton," Toby said. "But then you come in here with Miss Ivery and now you're doing this."

"Miss Ivery gave me no choice," Doc replied.

"I don't believe it," Toby said. "You could have turned her down. You didn't have to do it."

Doc put down the parchment.

"Toby," he said, taking the boy's shoulders. "We can't bring Jack Welton back. Can we?"

"No, I guess not."

"Then what do you want for the ranch?"

"I don't know."

"Do you want Johnny and Diana to come back and live here?" Doc asked. "Do you want them to have their rightful inheritance?"

"I guess so," he replied. "Who are you, mister?"

"A friend of Johnny's," Doc replied. "And if you want him to be the master of the Bar W again, you must let me do what I have to do."

"I don't understand," Toby said.

"You will in time," Doc replied. "Toby, will you trust me?"

"I guess I will," Toby rejoined. "But you shouldn't have done what you did with Miss Ivery. It wasn't right."

"I couldn't agree more," Doc said. "Now, Toby, if you will just put my suit on the bed and go outside the door."

"What do you want me to do out there?"

"Just knock on the door if someone is coming," Doc replied.

"All right," Toby said. "But I hope you know what you're doing, mister."

"So do I," Doc replied.

Toby went through the threshold, leaving Doc to unroll the first parchment from the marble-topped table. "Last Will and Testament of John Lincoln Welton" was printed at the

top of the page. The document left everything to Velma
Ivery Welton. It was signed by Jack Welton and the territorial justice. Sherman Ivery and his sister were the wit-
nesses. A calligrapher had done a neat job on the writing.
As far as Doc could see, the entire thing was in order.

CHAPTER TEN

Raider stood in front of the lodge, watching as Bronc Talbot's men formed a semicircle around him. Talbot was standing in the center of the gathering, an arrogant half-smile stretched across his tobacco-stained lips. When Raider saw a man as big and mean as Talbot, the first thing he asked himself was what he could do to hurt him. Raider had been ill prepared for the man's intimidating presence, but despite his grumbling stomach, he managed to remain unruffled on the outside.

"Am I in, or ain't I?" Raider asked.

"You think you can ride up here and throw in with us just like that?" Talbot replied.

"Why not?" Raider asked. "Either you need another gun or you don't. If you do, I stay. If not, I just ride out. No harm done. I been looking for work for a long time in these parts. You won't be the first un that's turned me away."

"What makes you think we need guns?" Talbot asked.

"From the looks of this bunch, you could use as many as you can get," Raider replied.

Talbot's boys didn't like that comment. But Raider had to push, to be as mean as they were, otherwise he didn't stand a chance of joining them. As he met Talbot's burning eyes, he tried to have faith in Doc's plan.

"You got a right smart mouth," Talbot said, dropping his hand toward his pistol butt. "Maybe I ought to teach you some manners."

Raider relaxed into his own stance, ready to meet Talbot's challenge.

"If we try it, one of us is bound to learn something the hard way," Raider said. "And one thing about learning the hard way, you never forget."

They might have shot it out in another moment, but Velma Ivery's regal entrance stopped them. She stepped between Raider and Talbot with her brother in her tracks. Her green eyes regarded Raider and then Talbot.

"What's going on here?" she asked.

"This boy says he wants to join up with us," Talbot replied. "I just told him we don't need nobody."

"What's your name, mister?" she asked.

"They call me Raider."

"And what makes you think we're in need of your services?" she asked.

"Ran into a man named Colter, two days south of here," Raider replied. "Said y'all was hiring for a cattle drive. Said y'all needed guns, what with Wounded Wolf on the loose."

"We don't need him," Talbot barked.

"I'll be the judge of that," she replied. "Tell me, Mr. Raider, can you shoot straight?"

"More than most, less than some," he replied.

"Less than me," Talbot rejoined. "That's for sure."

"Course, I ain't got thirty men to back me up," Raider said. "But if you want to try me alone, I'm ready right now."

Talbot hesitated. His men were whispering among themselves. Velma Ivery was smiling at him. Raider could tell from the gleam in her eyes that she would like nothing more than to see Talbot humiliated—or dead.

"Yeah, I didn't think you'd face me head on," Raider replied. "'Scuse me, ma'am. I'd best be riding out. Your big man there ain't got much liver."

Raider spun on his feet. He had counted on the rustling noise of Talbot's hand going for his pistol as soon as his back was turned. Raider wheeled around, aiming the .44 at his head before Talbot could draw. Talbot stood wide-eyed, his gun halfway out of his holster.

"I ought to drop you for pulling on me with my back turned," Raider said. "But I don't like to kill a man less'n he needs it."

"It appears you're no match for the stranger," said Velma Ivery.

"Hire him, Velma," said her brother.

"I should," she replied. "Why don't you just shoot him, Mr. Raider? He's got it coming."

"No ma'am," Raider said. "I'd just be obliged if he'd take out his pistol real slow-like and drop it on the ground."

"Do as he says," Velma Ivery commanded.

Talbot didn't like it, but he still tossed his pistol onto the ground. Velma Ivery was smiling as if she had personally done damage to him. Raider started backing slowly toward his mount, keeping the .44 trained on Talbot.

"If I ain't welcome, I'll just be ridin' on out of here," Raider said. "Sorry about the trouble, ma'am."

"Hold it," replied Miss Ivery. "I want to talk to you."

"Let him run," Talbot scowled. "He's a big man when he's got a gun in his hand. I bet he ain't nothing without it."

Raider stopped in his tracks.

"Maybe you'd like to match me fist for fist," he said.

"I'd certainly like to see that," said Sherman Ivery.

A confident smile spread across Talbot's brown lips.

"That'd suit me just fine," Talbot replied.

Raider holstered his pistol and unbuckled his gunbelt. The group gathered in a circle around them. Talbot's men were alive with anticipation. They had seen their boss out-drawn, but they believed that retribution would soon be served. Talbot had at least fifty pounds on Raider. Raider tossed his gunbelt to Sherman Ivery.

"Watch my back," he said to Mr. Ivery.

"I'm not very good with one of these things," he replied.

"Do as he says," his sister commanded. "And if any one of you move to help either man, my brother will shoot you."

"Must be nice to have a woman to protect you," Talbot mocked.

Raider stepped to the center of the circle, drawing a line with his foot in the dirt. He placed his toe on the mark and raised his fists. Talbot came right at him, not toeing the mark, throwing a roundhouse right that Raider easily avoided. Raider moved to the side, answering Talbot with a quick left that stung the ugly man's crooked nose.

The circle of men began to yell for their boss. Talbot kept coming, hard and mean, striking the air where Raider had just been. He may have been outweighed, but the bigger man was too slow. Riader kept up with the stinging left that reddened Talbot's face. Out of frustration, Talbot swung low, trying to catch Raider in the groin. But Raider stepped aside, coming back over the top with a hard right hand that struck Talbot on the temple. The big man staggered backward, falling to the ground. Blood was flowing from his mouth and nose as his men helped him up.

"You must want to git your back broke," Talbot cried.

He charged Raider, tackling him around the legs. Raider hit the dirt hard, feeling the breath leave his lungs. Talbot was all over him, trying to pin him with his superior weight. He put a knee in Raider's groin, stunning him even more. Talbot got on his feet and started kicking Raider with his boots. Raider was finally still, and Talbot eased up, thinking he was unconscious.

"You ain't so tough now, boy," Talbot said.

Suddenly Raider rolled toward the big man, throwing out his legs, tripping Talbot and sending him headlong into the dirt. Raider leapt to his feet and toed the mark again. Talbot couldn't believe Raider was up so quickly.

"Get up, hog-biscuit," Raider cried. "I'll tear your fat throat out."

"You must be wantin' to die, boy," Talbot sneered. "And I'm gonna oblige you."

Talbot pulled a recently honed hunting knife from his crusty boot. The silver edge glistened. Raider kept his eyes on the knife as Talbot circled around him, lashing out at Raider's midsection.

"I'm gonna make you a soprano, boy," Talbot said.

Talbot rushed him like a lancer, holding the knife in front of him. Raider remembered the tae-kwon-do that Doc had showed him. He grabbed Talbot's wrist and fell to one side, whipping Talbot into a roll on the ground. Talbot came up with the hunting knife sticking out of his forearm. He cried out, pulling the blade from the wound, setting off the stream of blood down his forearm.

"Kill him!" Talbot cried. "Somebody kill him now!"

Raider snatched his gunbelt from Sherman Ivery's smooth hand. He pulled the .44 out of the holster and brought it up cocked. Facing thirty men, he felt like *he* had swallowed a knife blade.

"I got six slugs," Raider said. "Let me see if there's six of you ready to die."

"Somebody help me," Talbot moaned. "Can't you see I'm bleedin'?"

"Get the doctor," said Velma Ivery.

As her brother started toward the lodge, Velma Ivery's green eyes fell on Raider's weary form.

"Impressive," she said. "Where did you learn to fight like that?"

"It just comes natural," replied Raider.

She raised a tender hand to the cut on Raider's forehead.

"I've been waiting for someone to teach him a lesson," she said. "I could use a man like you, mister."

Raider pulled her hand away from his face.

"If you don't mind, ma'am, I'll be moving on. That old boy there ain't gonna want to shake my hand after what we just been through. He might want to chop it off, but not shake it."

Doc rushed in, carrying his black bag. He avoided looking at Raider. He saw the knife wound in Talbot's forearm. Raider had certainly been up to his old tricks, Doc thought.

"Good God, what happened?" he asked.

"Mr. Talbot got more than he bargained for," replied Velma Ivery. "See what you can do about the arm and then attend to this gentleman."

"I'm okay," Raider said.

"Velma, may I speak to you for a moment?" said Sherman Ivery.

He pulled her aside, but not quite out of Raider's earshot. Raider put his hands over his head, as if he were working out a kink in his arms. He wasn't sure that he liked what he heard.

"I caught the doctor looking through the gun cabinet," said Sherman Ivery.

"So?" she replied. "Maybe he's interested in guns."

"I just don't like it," he said. "Two strangers show up on the same day. It just doesn't feel right to me."

"You worry too much, Sherman," she said in a chilling voice. "I have plans for the apothecary—and the new man, too."

Doc had finished the bandage on Talbot's arm. The big man staggered to his feet and looked Raider in the eye. Raider was ready to kill him if he had to.

"You ain't seen the last of me," Talbot said. "Best be lookin' over your shoulder. I'm gonna be there when you least expect it."

"You and the rest of your Indians?" Raider said.

"What?"

"Your man Colter talked a little more than he had to," Raider replied. "Know what I mean, Chief?"

"You're a dead man," Talbot said. "You hear me? Dead!"

He wheeled around and staggered through his gang of men. They followed on his heels like a loyal pack of hunting dogs. Raider sure as hell didn't like the odds of facing them by himself. He felt Velma Ivery's hand on his shoulder.

"Let the doctor take a look at you," she said.

"I don't need no sawbones," Raider replied. "Hell, they can kill you in two weeks."

"I have a tincture that will prevent infection," Doc said. "You'll have to come to my wagon."

"Go on," said Velma Ivery. "He won't hurt you."

"All right," Raider replied.

He did not want to seem too eager to talk to Doc.

"And I want to have a word with you as soon as you're

finished," said Velma Ivery. "I think I might have a job for you after all."

At the wagon, Raider flinched when Doc dabbed his cuts with an alcohol tincture.

"You got to use that hell-fire shit?" Raider groaned.

"Why did you pick a fight with Talbot?" Doc asked.

"That tub of guts," Raider replied. "Hell, it just happened. And I think that woman wanted me to fight him."

"If my guess is correct, she wants you to kill him," Doc replied. "We were wrong about the brother. He's simply a pawn."

"Got a bitty hen ruling the roost, eh?" Raider said. "Why would she want me to kill Talbot?"

"She loathes him," Doc replied. "And she's afraid that he's too firmly entrenched in here. He could stage a mutiny at any time. Velma Ivery and her brother would be out on their ears."

"Out on their asses would be more like it."

"Eloquently put."

"You want me to try to stay on?" Raider asked.

"No," Doc replied. "In fact, I want you to hit me."

"What?"

"Hit me," Doc replied. "Make for your horse. I'll see you tonight, at the base of the trail on the valley side of the ridge."

"Be careful," Raider said. "The brother caught you going through the gun cabinet."

"Hit me, damn it, Velma Ivery is coming this way."

Raider pulled his punch, but it still caught Doc squarely on the mouth. Doc tumbled backward. Raider bolted for his mount, leaping into the saddle from behind. He reared the horse and fled toward the southern pass into the valley. No one in Talbot's motley group bothered to chase him. Velma Ivery came rushing toward Doc, giving him a hand as he got up brushing his suit.

"What was that all about?" she asked.

"That brute disparaged your good name," Doc replied. "I can't tell you what he said because I am a gentleman.

But when I tried to make him take it back, he struck me and simply ran off."

"I could have used a man like him," she said. "He surely got the best of Bronc Talbot."

"Good riddance to him, I say," Doc replied. "Am I bleeding?"

"A little," she said. "Let's go inside. I'll take care of it for you. And your suit will have to be cleaned again."

"I'll have to take it off."

"Of course," she whispered. "I know something better than medicine.

Doc was sure she did.

CHAPTER ELEVEN

Doc thought Velma Ivery would never fall asleep. She kept after him for the better part of the night, as if she was determined to drain every ounce of his manly energies. Each time she showed signs of drifting off, she would renew her lustful posture, climbing to a pinnacle that forced Doc beyond the call of duty. Raider, thought Doc, would have been better suited to the lascivious task.

"You've never known a woman like me, have you?" she whispered.

"I can't say that I have," Doc gasped.

Beyond her animalistic gruntings and groanings, Velma Ivery offered no more unsolicited information about the workings of the ranch. She did commend Doc for patching up Bronc Talbot, even though she didn't care if Talbot dropped dead on the spot. Doc was inclined to agree with her on that score. The presence of Talbot and his crew made the task much more difficult and life-threatening.

"There aren't too many men like you in this territory, Mr. Weatherbee," she whispered on the pillow. "I wish it were more civilized out here."

"I concur," Doc replied, watching the rise and fall of her massive breasts. "But soft, rest we in nightshade. The sleep will revive us."

"You talk so pretty," she said. "I . . ."

Her breath diminished into a deep, low sigh. Doc made sure she was out of his arms before she fell asleep, not wanting to disturb her when he slipped out to meet Raider. Hopefully, he would be back before she awakened. And in the event of discovery, he could attribute his nightly sojourn to suspicious sounds outside the window. At any rate, it was certainly going to be a long night.

He lifted one leg over the bed and felt his foot hit the cold wooden floor. The night was much chillier than he would have imagined. Apparently the middle of September was like winter in the territory. After slipping into his clothes, Doc chose the window for his exit. He skirted around the side of the house and started for the east ridge on foot. He was walking for several minutes before he realized someone was following him.

It was no good having someone on his tail. He had but one choice—to waylay the pursuer and attribute the attack to the nighttime activities of Wounded Wolf. Even if he didn't kill the stalker, he would have to render him immobile, and that would require an overpowering blow. He hit the ground, lying on his stomach, waiting for the dark figure that came along behind him. When the shadow was upon him, he leapt to his feet, tackling the would-be assailant, raising his fist to strike. A girl's cry stopped him.

"Diana!" Doc said. "What the devil are you doing?"

"I was going to the ridge myself," Diana replied. "I saw you come out of *her* bedroom window so I followed you."

"Please," Doc said, helping her to her feet, "don't hold the widow against me. My . . . assignation with her was unavoidable."

"I'm sure it was," she replied with a note of petulant sarcasm in her voice.

"Diana, you must go back," Doc replied. "If both of us are discovered missing, Velma and her brother are liable to make the connection between us. His suspicions have already been aroused by the coincidental arrival of Raider and myself."

"I'm coming with you," she said. "I want to see my brother."

"Diana, please."

"We're wasting time," she replied. "I'm not going back, so we might as well start moving."

"I don't suppose it will do any good to argue," Doc said. "Let's hurry. I want to get back before we're missed."

They trod the damp, spongy ground to the edge of the ridge. Raider, Johnny, and Little Bright Wing were waiting for them at the base of the trail. Johnny hugged his sister and shook Doc's hand. He seemed excited.

"I'm ready to go, Doc," said Johnny. "When do we go in?"

"First things first, Johnny," Doc replied.

"Hell fire, Doc," Johnny said. "I'm ready to pay back Sherman Ivery for killin' my pa."

"I don't believe that Sherman Ivery killed your father," Doc replied.

"What?"

"He's rather ineffectual," Doc said. "Raider, didn't you hear him say that he was unschooled in the use of firearms?"

"That's right," Raider replied. "He didn't seem like no grizzly bear to me. More like a bear cub."

"Are you sayin' he's innocent?" Johnny cried.

"No, but he's merely a puppet of his sister," Doc said. "She's running the ranch. Although, I wonder..."

"I told you she was a bad one," Little Bright Wing rejoined.

"No!" Johnny insisted. "Sherman Ivery killed my pa. Who else could it have been?"

"I'm votin' for Talbot," Raider said. "He's ornery enough. He's a backshooter, too. If I hadn't been a step ahead of him, I'd be lyin' plugged-down in the ground right now."

"Talbot's a possibility," Doc replied. "Although, I'm not sure Velma Ivery could have done everything by herself. She loathes Talbot. And given the ineffectual nature of her brother, it follows that there's another accomplice somewhere behind the queen's gambit."

"Yeah, like who?" Johnny cried.

"The man in black, the man at Ivery's the day your pa was killed," Raider said.

"Precisely," Doc rejoined.

"I ain't buyin' it," Johnny said. "Sherman Ivery killed my pa, and I'll believe it till you prove otherwise."

"That's exactly what I intend to do," Doc replied.

An icy northwester rolled down the slope, chilling them, letting them know that summer was a memory. Johnny shook his head, turning his back to Doc and Raider. His sister put a hand on his shoulder.

"Johnny, weren't you telling me that we have to trust Doc and Raider?" she said.

"They're gonna be takin' the herd south," Johnny said. "In a couple of days, most likely. They're gonna sell the herd in Salt Lake City and we ain't gonna have nothin' to show for Pa's work."

"Yes, but . . ."

"But nothin'," Johnny railed. "I say we find our own men. I say we ride down on 'em and shoot the hell out of 'em. Take what's mine. That's what I say."

"There's easier ways to tree a polecat," Raider replied. "Now, I know you're riled up, boy, and I don't blame you. But we ain't gonna be stupid about this thing. You want to take us off the case, you say so right now. Otherwise, you do what we say."

Johnny turned away, snorting and fuming. His sister tried to mollify him. Doc took Raider aside.

"Well said, Raider," he replied.

"You find anything interesting in the gun cabinet?" Raider asked.

"I didn't have time to match the shell casing to the appropriate chamber," Doc replied. "Perhaps tomorrow. Your comment about the Indian raids certainly evoked Talbot's ire. I'd say he's responsible for the raids on the surrounding settlements."

"We figured that out already," Raider said. "You get anything new?"

"I uncovered something that may work against us," Doc said.

"What?" Johnny cried, overhearing them. "What did you find out?"

Doc had not intended to tell him right away.

"I managed to sneak a look at your father's last will and testament," Doc replied.

"Yeah? So?"

"He left everything, all of his holdings, to Velma Ivery," Doc replied. "And there were no provisions for you or your sister."

"That can't be right."

"The document was signed by your father himself, and it was verified by the territorial jurisprudence," Doc said.

"You're bamboozled, Doc," Johnny replied bitterly.

"I beg your pardon."

"My father never signed his name in his life," Johnny replied. "He couldn't even write. He made his mark when he had to sign something. He didn't sign no will."

"Well, that certainly sheds new light on this case," Doc said.

"What can you do?" Diana asked.

"We must wait," Doc replied. "Little Bright Wing, are you interested in going back to the Bar W?"

"Never!" she replied. "I ain't mixing it up with that sick bastard Ivery again."

"Well, I certainly can't force you," Doc said. "At any rate, Diana and I must return to the lodge. I'll leave tomorrow, and we'll rendezvous outside the valley. We'll have to head for Helena as soon as possible. I want to discuss this matter with the territorial jurisprudence before we move any further. I think we'll uncover a few other facts in Helena. Raider, does that sound right to you?"

"Seems like we ain't got much choice," Raider replied. "Less'n we take the law into our own hands."

"I say we do just that!" Johnny cried.

"We can't," Doc said.

"He's right, Johnny," Raider rejoined. "We got to go by

the book. A Pinkerton stands for the law. Sometimes I don't like it any better than you do. But we got to do right."

Johnny stormed up the trail, back to the ridge. The lad was headstrong, Doc thought, but he would stay in line as long as Raider kept an eye on him. Also, an attack on the Bar W would jeopardize his sister's safety, a fact that Johnny would realize when he calmed down.

"He'll be okay," Raider said.

"I hope so," Diana replied.

"We'll meet tomorrow on the other side of the ridge," Doc said. "I'll break away as soon as I can."

Raider and Little Bright Wing went up the trail, leaving Doc to escort Diana Welton back to the lodge. Along the way, Doc speculated as to Johnny's chances in a legal effort to recover his property. There was a nagging suspicion in the back of Doc's mind that made him think the road might be longer than he hoped.

"Thank you, Mr. Weatherbee," Diana said when they were in the shadow of the ranch house. "I'd like to apologize for my brother."

"That's quite all right."

She wrapped her arms around him and put her soft cheek on his shoulder.

"Hurry, dear girl," Doc said. "We mustn't be discovered."

When she disappeared around the corner of the house, Doc started for the bedroom window. He paused at the open casement, listening for Velma Ivery's heavy breathing. He didn't hear it. Before he could throw a leg over the windowsill, something rang through his skull, with a dull pain following. A blow had been delivered to his neck from behind. Doc fell backward, hitting the ground, losing consciousness, oblivious to the sudden goings-on around him....

Doc was freezing when he opened his eyes. He stared up at the sky, which was matted with low-hanging clouds against a purple scrim of half-light. When he ascertained that he was on his back, he tried to sit up. A sharp pain spread from his neck to his forehead. Lying still, he tried to assess what was damaged and what was numbed by the cold air of the Montana daybreak. As he slowly sat up, he saw that he had been lying in the back of his own wagon. The silhouette of a face stared down at him.

"I saved you," said a thin voice.

"Toby?"

"Yes, it's me, and I saved you from the men at the Bar W," he replied. "You want some whiskey?"

"I need something for my sore head," Doc replied.

Doc smelled the sweet, sickening fumes of the thick corn liquor in Toby's jug. He knew if he drank the cheap mash he'd have a painful stomach to match his head. After politely declining to drink, he began to mix a powder that would assuage most of the pain. Toby watched him with interest.

"You sure are smart to know about all that stuff," Toby said.

"No smarter than you," Doc replied. "You saved my life, Toby. How ever did you do it?"

"I was awake when you climbed out of Miss Ivery's window," Toby replied. "I sleep in the loft at the top of the stable. I got windows on all four sides. I can see everything from my bed. Nobody knows about it but me."

"Did you see them hit me when I came back?"

"I sure did," Toby replied. "Talbot snuck up on you. He hit you and then ran off. Just left you there. That's when I climbed down and came across the yard. I crawled under the house and hid. Talbot told Miss Ivery that he was gonna kill you as soon as he took care of the girl."

"I can imagine what that swine meant by that," Doc said.

"Why are they keepin' her locked up?"

"Ransom," Doc replied. "An old custom of war."

"You can get her out of there, Mr. Weatherbee."

"I'm glad you have such faith in me, my friend. My head is throbbing with evidence of my own ineptitude."

"You're my friend," Toby said. "You gave me candy, and you said you would help Johnny and Diana. Poor Diana! They locked her up. They ran off Johnny and now they've locked her up."

"Toby, how on earth did you manage to get me out of

there while I was unconscious?"

"I dragged you under the house," he replied. "You were asleep. When Talbot came back, I told him you had run off to the east. I said you had stole a horse. Miss Ivery told him to take every man and bring you back. She said you were the law, or something like that."

"I'm afraid she's on to me. A wily female, that one!"

"Are you going to let me finish my story?"

"Of course, Toby."

"Where was I?"

"The men had just run off to find me."

"Yes," Toby said. "All of them went off to find you. That's when I went to get your wagon. I hitched it up and drove it next to the house. Nobody even saw me when I put you in the back of the wagon and pulled that canvas over you."

"Commendable," Doc replied. "And no one saw you drive away?"

"Miss Velma saw me," Toby replied. "But I fooled her. She says: 'Toby, where you takin' that wagon?' So I says: 'Mr. Talbot told me to drive it out of the valley and burn it.' And then she says: 'Burn it to the ground.' So I drove it out here."

"Where are we?"

"On the other side of the east ridge," Toby replied.

"I've got to find Johnny and Raider," Doc said.

"Johnny's here?"

"Yes, he is, Toby, and so is my partner. We're Pinkerton operatives, and Johnny has hired us to investigate his father's death."

"I knew you were something like that," Toby replied.

"You're very clever, Toby," Doc said. "Thanks for saving my life."

"Mr. Weatherbee?"

"Yes, Toby?"

"Can I have another piece of candy?"

"Of course you can, Toby. Of course you can."

CHAPTER TWELVE

"I'm going down there after my sister!" cried Johnny Welton.

Doc and Toby had found them easily. When Doc told Johnny about Diana's imprisonment, he went berserk. Little Bright Wing and Toby were hiding behind Raider as Johnny railed.

"Doc, you and Raider can come with me if you want to. It don't make no never mind to me. You can go straight to hell for all I care, but I'm going after my sister!"

"That's exactly what they want," Doc replied. "They'll kill you and Diana and us too if we aren't careful."

"You think they're gonna just let you waltz in there and take your sister out?" Raider asked. "You're might plucky yourself, but you ain't no match for Talbot and his gang, Johnny. You'd never make it to the lodge—even with us backing you up."

"Drop the case if you can't stand behind me," Johnny cried.

"We *are* behind you," Doc replied. "But you have to cooperate. We need you to solve this case, Johnny."

"You're just tellin' me that so I won't do what I know is right," Johnny replied.

"Shit fire, then," Raider said. "Let him ride down there and git his ass shot off."

"Raider, I don't think that's the way to convince him."

"No, I mean it, Doc," Raider persisted. "If he wants to be stupid, let him do it on his own. Go ahead, be a little shit-bird. But don't expect me to hang around and watch it."

Raider's tone carried with it a certain finality that settled in over the group. Johnny fumed for another half hour, kicking the ground and looking down toward the lodge. He knew Raider was right, but it took him a few minutes for his pride to shrink.

"All right," he said. "What do you need me for, Doc?"

"To guide us to Helena," Doc replied.

"Helena?"

"It's the territorial seat of justice," Doc replied.

"That supposed to be funny or somethin'?" Johnny asked.

"It's your only hope, Johnny," Doc replied. "Legal recourse. We'll present our findings to the judge and pursue the due process of the law."

"What if the law ain't in my favor?"

"Then we will file a complaint with the marshal or perhaps the local Army command," Doc said. "If all else fails, we will return here and pursue the case on our own."

"I ain't even sure I can pay you," Johnny replied.

"I got sixty-five dollars, Johnny," Toby chimed in.

"You take that money and go to Bishop's Mill," Johnny replied. "I don't want you gettin' hurt, Toby. Stay there till I come for you."

"Sure, I'll go, Johnny, if that's what you want," Toby said.

"We're willing to stay on the case," Doc rejoined. "But if you want us out, say so now."

Johnny glanced back and forth between them.

"You two are some pair," Johnny said. "I git the feelin' that you could talk the devil out of hell if you had to."

"It's something that we've learned to live with," Doc replied.

"What'll it be, kid?" Raider asked.

"Helena," Johnny replied. "But I want to be back here

as soon as we can. I want to be here when Talbot tries to take the herd out."

"What you got in mind?" Raider asked.

"Making them pay," Johnny replied. "Making them pay for all of this."

"Don't forget what the Good Book says," Raider said.

"I know," Johnny replied. "'Vengeance is mine.'"

"'Sayeth the Lord,'" Doc rejoined.

"It will be," Johnny said coldly. "It will be."

Little Bright Wing's muffled cry woke Raider just before dawn. He sat up, bringing his pistol with him. They had camped the night before in a stand of juniper trees, one day's ride from the Bar W, just beyond the Little Belt Mountains. Raider wasn't ready for what he saw in the misty sheen of daybreak. He knew his gun would be useless.

"We got company," he said to rouse Doc and Johnny.

Wounded Wolf was sitting on Doc's wagon with his arms folded across his thick chest. Little Bright Wing had been bound and gagged. She was standing in front of her husband, restrained by two Sioux braves. Eight more warriors surrounded the encampment. They held shiny new Remington repeaters that glinted in the shafts of new light between the gnarled junipers.

"It appears the estrangement is over," Doc said. "The bride and groom are reunited."

"This ain't no time to be funny," Raider said. "We're just as good as meat on a spit."

"He ain't gonna kill us," Johnny said.

"You sure about that?" Raider replied.

"Remember Palmer?" Johnny asked. "If he wanted us dead, we would be bleedin'."

"He's a big son of a bitch," Raider said. "How come he don't take the girl and just vamoose?"

"I sure as hell don't know that," Johnny replied.

Wounded Wolf extended his corded arms over Little Bright Wing and spoke in a deep, ghostly voice that reverberated through the forest. After a rasping, guttural dialogue, one of the warriors reached down to pull the gag from Little Bright Wing's mouth. She replied to him in the same language and then listened as her husband spoke again. When he was finished, she turned to Doc and Raider.

"He doesn't speak the white man's language," Little Bright Wing said. "He wants to talk to you through me."

"Perfectly acceptable," Doc said.

"Talk is better than torture or death," Raider rejoined.

As Wounded Wolf spoke, he looked straight ahead, disregarding the presence of everyone but himself. He gestured with his rippling arms, provoking a sharp pain in Raider's gut. Ice danced along Doc's spine, attributable to the savage discourse.

"He wants to trade for me," Little Bright Wing said finally.

"Trade? But you're his already," Raider replied.

"He says you own me now," she said. "But he can't kill you because I told him that you did not steal me from him. He knows I left on my own, so he thinks he has to trade for me now."

"Ask him what he's got to trade?" Johnny asked.

Wounded Wolf peered down at Johnny when he heard his voice. Johnny was frozen in his tracks. He didn't like the way Wounded Wolf stared at him. Doc thought he saw recognition in those dark eyes.

"We can't trade for her like she's a side of beef," Raider said. "That's inhuman."

"I don't think we should insult this man," Doc replied.

"Little Bright Wing, do you want to go back to the reservation with him?" Raider asked.

"It doesn't make any difference," she replied. "You'd better make a deal with him. He'll only kill you if you don't. My husband is used to having things his way. Don't worry about me. Save your own asses, pronto."

"Practical girl," Doc said.

"She just wants to keep livin' too," Johnny replied.

"He could just kill us and take her," Raider said.

"Don't give him any ideas," Doc rejoined.

"Injuns got honor too," Johnny said.

"Ask him if he still has my mule," Doc said.

Little Bright Wing's tone was less harsh as she spoke the language. Wounded Wolf jumped off the Studebaker and clapped his hands together. One of his warriors bolted into the trees, only to return with Judith on a tether. Doc wanted to throw his arms around the animal's beloved neck, but he managed to restrain himself.

"Don't that beat all," Raider said.

"They were going to eat her," Little Bright Wing said.

"Tell him he has a bargain," Doc cried.

Little Bright Wing nodded at her husband. He grabbed the tether and handed it to Doc. Doc patted Judith's muzzle as she brayed. He tried not to be too jubilant in front of Little Bright Wing. As much as he was happy to see Judith again, he hated to see the girl getting the bad end of things.

"I wish this could have worked out better," Doc said.

"I got some shit luck," Little Bright Wing replied. "But don't cry over me, dandy. They ain't gonna kill me."

Wounded Wolf came toward them. He stood in front of Johnny, glaring into his face. His savage hand knocked away the hair that hung over half of Johnny's countenance. Again he called to his wife in his native tongue.

"He wants to know if you are the son of the Bear," Little Bright Wing said.

"Yes, I guess I am," Johnny replied.

Wounded Wolf did not wait for his wife to translate. He spoke again, all the time keeping his eyes on Johnny.

"He says you must look at Three Rocks of the Sun," Little Bright Wing said.

"Why?" Johnny asked.

"He says you will find the Bear," Little Bright Wing replied. "The Bear, who was friend to the Sioux."

Wounded Wolf gestured toward the trees. Two of his warriors whisked Little Bright Wing into the forest, disappearing like foxes carrying their kill. Wounded Wolf erupted with a sharp cry and followed the rest of his party into the trees. In less than thirty seconds, all traces of the Indians were gone.

"It's like they were never here," Raider said.

"That was certainly an unnerving way to start the morning," Doc said. "Although I prefer it to dying."

"What was all that stuff about rocks and bears?" Raider asked.

"Three Rocks of the Sun is north of here," Johnny replied. "It has something to do with Indian medicine."

"And the Bear?" Doc asked.

Johnny sighed and shook his head.

"They used to call my pa the Bear," Johnny replied. "He used to wear a bearskin coat. Ever'body thought he looked like a bear when he put it on, because he was so big and all."

"Do you think Wounded Wolf knew your father?" Doc asked.

"Maybe," Johnny replied. "I know Pa had dealings with the Sioux. One winter he gave Gray Wolf ten head of cattle for the tribe. The elk herd was poor that year, so Pa gave beef to anybody that came along."

"What do you say, Doc?" Raider asked.

"I don't know," Doc replied. "Johnny, do you think we should take a look at this Three Rocks place?"

"It's a half day's ride," Johnny said. "It'll take us off the trail for a while, but I don't care. If you want to go on, I can meet you in Helena."

"I say we stick together," Raider replied.

"A sentiment that I endorse," Doc rejoined. "Shall we forge ahead, Johnny?"

"You're happy all of a sudden," Raider said to Doc. "We almost lost our scalps to Wounded Wolf."

"I'm aware of that," Doc replied. "I'm thankful to be alive."

"You're just glad to have that mangy critter back," Raider accused. "She should have been dinner for the tribe."

But Raider couldn't wipe the smile from Doc's face. Things were back on course, Doc thought. Fortune had turned away death in the form of Wounded Wolf. And how bad could it be if Judith was back in the harness of the Studebaker?

• • •

In the middle of the plateau called Three Rocks of the Sun stood a single Sioux burial platform. The aboveground gravesite had been erected on thin poles made of saplings in order to prevent scavengers from climbing up onto the structure. Doc, Raider, and Johnny stared up at the primitive shrine. Johnny didn't want to admit what Doc and Raider suspected.

"That could be your father up there," Doc said.

"I ain't never heard of any Sioux burying a white man in one of their graves," Johnny said. "That ain't my pa."

"Maybe this is Wounded Wolf's idea of a joke," Raider offered.

"Well, somebody has to take a look," Doc replied. "Or we've wasted half a day for nothing."

"I'm tellin' you, it ain't my pa," Johnny insisted, turning his back to the grave.

But Doc had to see for himself. He pulled the wagon next to the platform and climbed up on the driver's seat. The first thing he saw was the fur coat draped over the body. Judging by the corpse, the man had been big. As big as a bear.

"Did this belong to your father?" Doc asked, holding up the coat for Johnny to see.

"Give me that!" Johnny cried.

Doc tossed the coat to Johnny, who inspected it carefully. He was fighting back the urge to cry. Raider felt damned sorry for the kid. Sometimes it was tough to face the truth.

"This was his coat," Johnny said softly. "Damn them. Damn them all. Those bastards will pay."

"Easy, boy," Raider rejoined.

Doc climbed down and took Raider aside.

"There's a hole the size of your fist in the chest of the body," Doc said.

"Shot with a large-caliber rifle from long range," Raider replied. "Just like we thought."

"I wondered why they buried him in an Indian grave," Doc said.

"Maybe out of respect," Raider offered. "The Sioux have been cheated so much they're bound to remember anything good that was dealt to them."

"Mr. Welton must have been an extraordinary man," Doc said.

"Think we should take the body with us to Helena?" Raider asked.

"We know where to find it," Doc replied. "It might disappear if we offer it as evidence too soon."

"Why do you say that?"

"Call it a hunch."

"I'm the one who's s'posed to get the hunches," Raider said. "Hell, you're right, though. Probably is safer here, what with Wounded Wolf ridin' wild-asses all over Creation."

"Keep an eye on our young friend there," Doc replied. "He's going to brood for a while."

"Can't say as I blame him."

"We're getting closer to the core of the trouble," Doc said. "It may not seem that way, but we are. If we have any luck at all, we'll uncover some evidence in Helena."

"I hope you're right."

"Johnny," Doc called. "Do you still have the key that your sister gave you? The one that seemed to be from the strongbox?"

"Yes, I do," Johnny replied. "I had forgotten about it."

"One more mystery that can be solved in Helena," Doc said.

"Let's ride," Johnny said.

He pulled his father's coat over his shoulders and jumped into the saddle. Johnny looked like a bear himself, Raider thought. And with the hateful gleam in his eyes, he was just as dangerous.

CHAPTER THIRTEEN

Helena, according to Fletcher Greeves, the Montana terri-
rorial justice, was not exactly known for the refined or
genteel manner of the town's inhabitants. It was a rough,
barren mining community, raised on the gold rush and sheer
will from colorless tents and lean-tos. As Doc had witnessed
on the way into Helena, the place still lacked primary hues.
Wooden dwellings that accounted for several guttings by
fire washed into a reddish-brown landscape that made Doc
want to be anywhere but Fletcher Greeves's dingy office.

"There's a tree at the edge of town," said the aging judge.
"Hanging tree, Mr. Weatherbee."

Doc had introduced himself as a lawyer from the East
who was hoping to make a home for himself in Montana.

"Used to be two kinds of justice in this territory," Greeves
said. "Whippin' and hangin'. These days the governor wants
me to put more men in prison. Have to take them all the
way down to Wyoming. Things are getting softer. I bet I
ain't hung ten men this year. Now the town council's thinkin'
about cuttin' it down."

In his black suit and white shirt, the gray-haired mag-
istrate looked more like a Puritan minister about to ring out
a congregation of lame sinners. His voice rose and fell in
a singsong delivery. Doc had come alone, leaving Raider

and Johnny at the Sundowner Hotel on Main Street.

"I take it you've been in the territory for quite a long time," Doc said.

"Sonny boy," Greeves replied. "I hunted buffalo with Bill Cody on the Missouri plateau."

Greeves turned away from his desk and pointed to a huge map of the territory that covered his wall.

"I trapped the eastern forests and the Musselshell River when I was just a boy."

"Where is that?" Doc asked, gazing up at the map.

"Let's get a closer look," Greeves said. "Step up here."

A self-satisfied smirk on his thin face indicated the pleasure he was deriving from his talk with Doc. He wanted to impress on a fellow barrister his importance in the scheme of territorial jurisprudence. His weathered finger traced a line across the central part of Montana, near the Elk Lodge Valley.

"You see it there?" Greeves asked.

Doc saw exactly what he wanted to see. A new line had been added to the map in black ink. It was broad, with smaller lines crossed through it—the usual symbol for a railroad track. Greeves put his hand on Doc's shoulder and turned him away.

"Lot of Easterners come out here," Greeves said. "My pappy did. Don't know how much work there'll be for a lawyer like yourself."

"Well," Doc said, sitting again, "I've already come upon a case that requires my attention."

"Well, good for you, son, good for you."

"Yes, I'm representing a young man named Johnny Welton," Doc said. "Do you know him, Your Honor?"

Greeves was ashen. He shook his head after a moment. Doc had caught him off guard, but he seemed to recover quickly.

"You mean you don't know the boy's family?" Doc asked.

"Can't say as I do," Greeves replied, the joker's smirk in place again on his thin lips.

"That's odd," Doc replied. "I saw a copy of Jack Welton's last will and testament. You had signed it yourself as the legal correspondent. It left everything to Velma Ivery Welton, Jack's second wife."

"So?"

"Well, doesn't it seem strange that the father didn't leave a thing to my client, his only son? That's why I came to see you, to find out if you could shed some light on Jack Welton's oversight."

Greeves stood up. He paced a little behind his desk. He moved with remarkable dexterity for an older man.

"Any thoughts or revelations?" Doc asked.

Greeves turned to him. He was no longer smiling. His voice took on a formal note.

"Partner, do you really expect me to remember every tinhorn and trapper that rides in here with a paper for me to make legal?"

"You would remember Jack Welton," Doc replied. "Tall—as big as a bear. He would have had a woman with him. Pretty, with dark hair, the kind of lady that doesn't turn up much out here."

"A woman?" he said too quickly. "Yes, I seem to..."

"Green eyes that could kill you," Doc replied.

Greeves raised a gray eyebrow.

"Yes, she did come in here with a man."

"Good," Doc said. "Do you remember if the man signed anything?"

"Now, he must have signed it if I made it legal," Greeves replied. "Wouldn't seem right if I made something legal that wasn't signed in front of me."

"No, it wouldn't seem right at all," Doc said. "There's just one small discrepancy. My client claimed his father couldn't write at all. Not even to sign his name. Is it possible, Your Honor, that a false party presented himself to you for verification of Jack Welton's will?"

"Are you callin' me a thief?" Greeves asked.

"No, sir," Doc replied. "If someone misrepresented himself to you, you couldn't be held responsbible for anything."

"Well, that ain't happened," Greeves said curtly. "I been a judge for eight years. I was appointed by the governor himself. No man has swindled me since I been in office.

Do you understand that, Mr. Yankee Lawyer?"

"Of course," Doc replied. "Never think for a moment that I would question your competence or integrity. I'll drop Johnny Welton's complaint immediately."

Greeves softened instantly. He smiled and leaned back in his chair. Doc asked if he had any further advice for a lawyer starting out in the territory.

"Don't go cobbin' around after every snot-nosed brat whose pappy decided to put him out of his will," Greeves replied. "You can get yourself into a lot of trouble by gettin' messed up with the wrong hombres in this town, sir."

"Of course," Doc said. "Perhaps I'll head east as soon as possible. Would you agree?"

"Goodbye, Mr. Weatherbee," Greeves said. "Just remember, anything I make legal in these parts stays legal."

"Good day to you, Your Honor."

Doc ran from the judge's office to the Sundowner Hotel. He was brimming with the need to unfold his thoughts and deductions for Raider's tough, discerning opinion. A note from his partner was leaning against the water pitcher. "Gone to Fargo office to check key," was all it said. It didn't matter to Doc. He could make a few stops himself. He wanted to get off a cable to Pinkerton headquarters in Chicago. And he hoped to pay a call on Mr. Reginald Barrow of the St. Paul Railroad Company before he told it all to Raider.

"Put down that pistol," Doc cried.

Doc had burst so abruptly into the room at the Sundowner that Raider had pulled his .44 out of its holster.

"I'm half tempted to shoot you for scaring us half to death," Raider growled.

"Just lower that hand cannon and don't say another word," Doc replied.

Raider recognized the tone of Doc's voice.

"But Doc," Johnny started, "don't you want to hear about the Wells Fargo office?"

"Better let him talk," Raider replied. "He's got that look in his eyes. You've figured it all out, ain't you, Doc?"

"You know me better than my own father," Doc replied.

Doc began to pace up and down. Johnny watched him, wondering why he was suddenly quiet. Raider knew he was just searching for a starting point. Doc whirled unexpectedly on his feet and pointed a finger at Johnny.

"Young man, I propose this. Velma Ivery and her brother conspired to murder your father and cheat you out of your inheritance."

"I know that."

"Let me finish. The Iverys are obvious, but a few things don't fit. First, who would hire such a man as Talbot? Not Sherman Ivery or his sister. No, a man who could link up with Talbot would have to be familiar with the criminal populace in this part of the country. I suspected that another conspirator existed. Today I discovered that third scoundrel. His name is Fletcher Greeves, and he's the territorial judge for this region."

"Shit, Doc," Raider said. "Where did you pull that one out of?"

"I don't believe it," Johnny rejoined.

"Hear me out," Doc insisted. "Do you agree that your father's will was faked, Johnny?"

"It had to be," Johnny replied. "I told you he couldn't write."

"Yet I saw the will at the ranch, and it bore a signature that was verified by Fletcher Greeves to be the signature of your father," Doc said. "In order to make everything legal, Velma Ivery purchased the services of the territory's highest-ranking justice. I'd be willing to bet that she threw herself into the pot to sweeten the bargain."

"That's a right serious charge," Raider said. "You know how the boss feels about gettin' mixed up in politics."

"Fletcher Greeves is not a politician," Doc replied. "He's a suspect in a murder conspiracy and a conspiracy to commit fraud through forged documents."

"Keep talkin'," Johnny said. "This is soundin' better."

"When I confronted Greeves about your father's will, he claimed at first to have no knowledge of it," Doc replied. "Even when I pushed him, he claimed only a vague recollection. Yet your father was a well-known man in these parts. Surely Greeves would have remembered him. And as soon as I told Greeves I was dissociating myself from your case, he seemed relieved."

"There's no chance he was just fooled by the Iverys?" Raider asked. "I mean—"

"Wait until I've finished," Doc replied. "I considered the same thing, Raider, until I looked in on a man named Reginald Barrow."

"Who?"

"A representative of the St. Paul Railroad," Doc replied. "The surveyor at the ridge gave me his name. Here, I want you to look at this map."

Doc pulled the folded paper from his coat pocket and spread it out on the bed.

"This map shows the railroad lines in this region," Doc said. "The existing ones are marked in black, the proposed lines are red. Do you see this red line here, Johnny? It goes right into the plains of central Montana, coming up from the south. It's only seven miles east of the Bar W."

"What does that mean?" Johnny asked.

"The same line appears on the map in the judge's office," Doc replied. "He knows about the line before it has appeared on any other maps of the area."

"So maybe the railroad was showin' him where they were gonna put the track," Raider offered. "You know how that legal stuff can get. Maybe the judge advised them about something."

"Let me get this out," Doc said. "Now, on the day that your father was killed, he rode out to meet the representatives of the St. Paul Railroad."

"How do you know that?" Johnny asked.

"Because Mr. Barrow verified the appointment," Doc replied. "He had several gentlemen with him who will testify to that fact. They discussed the purchase of beef for their crews and the purchase of the land shown there on the map."

"Pa didn't own that land," Johnny said.

"Apparently he did," Doc replied. "He must have been secretive about his business dealings. What Little Bright

Wing witnessed was a short business meeting of your father and his associates."

"He never told nobody about none of it," Johnny said.

"But how does this connect the Iverys and Greeves?" Raider asked.

"Good question," Doc replied. "First, let's look at the evidence the way Little Bright Wing described it to us at Reva's. After the men left your father, he climbed off his horse and considered their offer. He had no reason to suspect that someone was waiting for him in the rocks on the slope of the ridge. A man with a large-caliber rifle. I think that man was Fletcher Greeves."

"A judge?" Johnny cried.

"Little Bright Wing said she saw a man in black with Ivery on the same day your father was killed," Doc replied. "He could have preceded her to the ridge and fled back to the other ranch."

"Could he handle a buffalo rifle?" Raider asked.

"He's old, but he's spry," Doc replied. "He admitted to me that he used to hunt buffalo. That gives him a knowledge of firearms."

"But why would a judge want to kill my pa?" Johnny asked.

"Because he's in cahoots with Velma Ivery," Doc replied. "You see, according to Barrow, the tracks coming into the Montana cattle country stand to benefit the Bar W in two ways. Since your father owned the land that the railroad wanted, whoever inherited the land would get the proceeds from the sale. Furthermore, the grazing acreage of the Bar W would produce plenty of cattle to ship to southern markets by rail. Can you imagine what Greeves thought when the widow whispered that sweet poison in his ear?"

"We need proof," Raider said.

"I would never have found it if I hadn't gone to see Barrow," Doc replied. "After your father disappeared and the will was filed, the railroad came to Velma Ivery with an offer on the land. She told them to negotiate with her legal representative, Fletcher Greeves. The old boy doubled the price. The railroad people are thinking about heading farther east to find a route."

"You sure dug up a smelly bag of bones, Doc," Raider said. "Maybe you can figure it in with what we found at the Wells Fargo office today."

"You had some luck?"

"I was tryin' to tell you," Johnny said. "My pa had left a strongbox there in my name. This was in it."

Johnny handed Doc a folded piece of paper and a hunk of greenish stone. Doc looked at the crusty parchment, which turned out to be a claim for mining. The claim had not been dated yet, which meant that it had not been filed officially. Doc hefted the stone and examined it closely.

"Why would Pa leave a worthless claim?" Johnny asked.

"What makes you think the claim is worthless?" Doc replied.

"But the gold rush is over."

"The surveyor had been working for some of the silver mines," Doc replied. "Did you know that silver ore often appears greenish when found in certain forms of rock?"

"A silver mine?" Raider said.

"At least a small deposit, judging by this sample," Doc replied. "Your father was smart, Johnny. He made sure Velma Ivery couldn't steal everything from you."

"You hatchin' some plan for all of this?" Raider asked.

"We're going to use the claim for bait," Doc replied. "Johnny has to file it with the assay office. Greeves will find out, because Johnny will spread it all over town that he's hit the mother lode. If Greeves is corrupt, he'll take measures to grab the claim away from Johnny. His power as a judge makes it easy for him to change legal documents. If Greeves shows up at the Bar W, we'll know he's our man."

"I got to hand it to you, Doc," Raider said. "It's all there. If you're right, what can we do? Greeves is the law in these parts."

"He reminded me of that," Doc replied. "We should set

the trap first and see if he falls into it. Johnny, do you know where this claim is located?"

"Yeah, up by Big Snowy," Johnny said. "I looked it up on the map in the Wells Fargo office."

"Excellent," Doc replied. "That's essential to our plan."

"How are we gonna fight Greeves?" Johnny asked.

"We file a report with our home office and the office of the territorial governor. Benjamin Potts, I believe."

"I hope this works," Johnny said.

He looked down at the ore in his hands.

"What is it?" Doc asked.

"My pa always said I'd be a rich man," Johnny said. "Now I know what he meant."

"Come on," Raider said. "Let's go catch us a bush-whackin' judge."

CHAPTER FOURTEEN

They rode hard through the Montana night, stopping only
to sleep a few hours just before dawn. Doc had left Judith
and the wagon in a stable in Helena. The Studebaker would
have slowed them down, and Doc wanted to reach the Elk
Lodge Valley by the following evening. He wanted to be
waiting for Fletcher Greeves. For something as important
as a silver claim, the mastermind would want to be on hand
himself.

They approached the east ridge in the cover of darkness.
Sentries were posted at the entrance to the valley. They
could see their fires burning. Raider wished he could be
near a fire, to stave off the icy night chill. He had purchased
a woolen coat in Helena, but it didn't fight off the bitter
wind that cut through the plain.

"How we gonna get up on the ridge?" Raider asked.

"Well, we can't go up where we were," Johnny replied.
"I know a way from the north."

"Will we be able to see the ranch house from there?"
Doc asked.

"Yeah, better than the other side," Johnny replied.

"Can they see us?" Raider asked.

"No, but we can't see the pass," Johnny replied. "The
view is blocked by the rocks."

166

"Can we see the road?" Doc asked.

"Yes."

"That's enough," Doc replied. "Now I suggest we go up and get some sleep."

"I hope we don't freeze to death," Raider said.

"Cold weather means the herd will be moving soon," Johnny said. "If they get the herd to market, my sister and me lose everything."

"What are you gettin' at?" Raider asked.

"I say we get our own men and ride down on 'em," Johnny replied. "It ain't too late to take back what's mine."

"I thought we discussed that already," Doc said. "Are you going to get hotheaded again?"

"Is it hotheaded to want my ranch back?" Johnny cried.

"Johnny, we are concerned with accumulating enough evidence to convict the murderers of your father," Doc replied. "If we are successful, you will have your property returned to you."

"You got the evidence already," Johnny said. "It ain't done us no good so far. They still got the Bar W, and I got nothin'."

"All right, boy," Raider said. "That's enough. Don't get out of line or I might have to take you down a peg. Doc and me have come too far for you to screw this up."

"Raider . . ."

Doc shook his head. He didn't want Johnny to become any more enraged. The kid had enough reason to be mad without Raider goading him. Doc turned toward Johnny.

"If Greeves shows here, as I think he will, then we will file a report with our agency and the territorial governor. The Pinkerton agency will stand behind you one hundred percent."

"The law?" Johnny said bitterly. "You see what the law has done. Fletcher Greeves is the law. Look at him."

"He won't be the law for long if Doc is right," Raider replied.

"We just have to wait, Johnny," Doc said.

Raider didn't like the look in Johnny Welton's eyes. Vengeance could do strange things to a man. The vengeful mind could be unpredictable and violent, especially in a young man who thought he was right.

"You gonna make it, Johnny?" Raider asked.

"Don't worry about me, Raider," Johnny replied. "I'm waitin'. And if Greeves don't show, then you and Doc can leave. I'll take over then. You won't be responsible."

"If I'm right," said Doc. "We won't have to wait long."

They walked slowly in the darkness toward the looming shadow of the east ridge.

After waiting all morning, Johnny was getting antsy. He complained and argued about everything, so much so that Raider was about to shut him up when a rider came into view. An Appaloosa mare pounded the road, throwing clumps of rich earth to all sides as it galloped toward the lodge. Raider raised Doc's spyglass to his eye.

"It's Greeves," Raider said. "Black suit and all."

"Let me see," Johnny replied. "Yep, it's him. You were right, Doc. I'm sorry."

"We'll have time for apologies later," Doc said. "I want you to ride to Big Snowy, Johnny. Find a hidden spot near the claim site and watch for anyone who arrives. If Greeves and his men come to the claim, simply observe them and head back immediately."

"I'll take my Sharps," Johnny replied.

"Leave it," Raider said. "We don't want you doin' nothin' stupid. Just take a look and ride on back here pronto."

"What if they see me?" Johnny asked.

"Run like hell," Raider replied. "Hell, you're sneakier than an Injun when you want to be."

"If you don't have a weapon, you won't be tempted to do anything rash," Doc rejoined.

"Hell, Doc . . ."

"Git gone, boy," Raider barked.

Johnny walked his horse down to the plain and headed northeast.

"You think he's gonna blow his stack?" Raider asked.

"Not if we respect him," Doc replied.

He lifted his glass to his eye, peering toward the lodge.

The group of bivouacked men had stirred and were forming a line in front of the house. Greeves was climbing onto a fresh horse.

"He's not wasting any time," Doc said. "Ivery's coming out of the house. He's going with them. Greeves looks like he's leading the way."

"What about the woman?"

"I don't see her," Doc replied.

"You really think it's gonna do any good to file a report with the governor's office?" Raider asked.

"That's Johnny's only legal recourse," Doc replied. "And I daresay our evidence will not be ignored."

"I still don't like it," Raider said. "Could get nasty, goin' after a gover'ment official."

"We have to tell the truth, Raider."

"Yeah, I guess so."

Raider's gut was stirring. The whole thing suddenly didn't feel right. His rumbling stomach made noises that reached Doc's ears. Doc looked sideways at his partner.

"Your abdomen is talking again," Doc said.

"I know."

"I don't like it when your stomach growls," Doc replied.

"Hell, Doc, what can go wrong? We wait for Johnny and scoot out of here as soon as he gets back. If we ride hard, they won't be able to catch us, even if they spot us. We write our report and the case is over."

"Yes, I know," Doc replied. "But I still don't like it when your stomach growls. It's my only superstition. When I hear that noise, it means that strange things can happen."

"Well," Raider said. "Let's hope you're wrong this time."

Three hours later, Greeves arrived back at the lodge. Doc peered through his glass, counting the number of men who came back with him. If Doc had figured correctly, Greeves had left three men guarding the claim. At least Johnny wasn't with the returning men, which meant he hadn't been captured. Sherman Ivery wasn't visible in the group either.

"Think Ivery stayed behind at the claim?" Raider asked.

"He wouldn't volunteer to guard it overnight," Doc replied. "Perhaps he wanted to dig out some ore for himself."

"Maybe he stayed behind to bury a careless kid," Raider offered. "Hell, I should have gone instead of Johnny."

"We shall see," Doc replied.

It was almost dark when they heard the scuffling of feet on the patch below them. Raider filled his hand with the .44. Doc produced his .38 Diamondback from his coat pocket. Johnny Welton came up the path with Sherman Ivery beside him.

"Son of a bitch!" Raider said.

"Look what I caught," Johnny called.

Ivery's soft hands were lashed behind him with a strip of rawhide. Johnny held an ivory-handled Colt .32 that obviously had belonged to his captive before Johnny took it away. Doc held out his hand.

"Give me the gun, Johnny," he said.

Johnny put the barrel to Ivery's temple.

"I can't do it, Doc," Johnny said. "He'll get away. I caught him good. When he stayed behind, I waited and jumped him on the slope."

"He's a maniac," Ivery whimpered.

"Looks like he roughed you up," Raider said.

Blood covered Ivery's shearling coat. Johnny had darkened his eyes and opened up cuts on his lips and forehead. Doc tried to take a step forward, but Johnny thumbed back the hammer on the Colt.

"You can't kill him," Doc said.

"He killed my pa," Johnny replied. "Why can't I kill him?"

"I didn't kill Jack Welton," Ivery cried. "It was that Indian, Wounded Wolf. My sister even got a letter from the Indian agent. I'm telling you, I didn't do it."

"Bullshit!" Johnny cried. "Bullshit!"

"Johnny," said Doc. "If I can prove he didn't kill your father, will you believe me?"

"How you gonna prove it?" Johnny asked.

"Let me show you," Doc replied.

"Hold steady, son," Raider said. "Listen to Doc."

"All right," Johnny said. "Prove it."

Doc reached down and picked up the Sharps that Johnny had left behind. He held up the rifle and a brass cartridge and then took a step toward Johnny. Johnny moved backward.

"What the hell are you doin', Doc?" he asked.

"Your father was killed with a large-caliber rifle," Doc replied. "I proved that with the surveyor's lens, and then I saw the proof at the burial ground."

"So?"

"Just step away and let Ivery come a little closer," Doc said. "Then I can prove he didn't kill your father. Go ahead, keep the pistol on him if you want to."

Johnny stepped back, allowing Ivery to come forward. Doc put the rifle at Ivery's feet and then handed him the cartridge. Johnny aimed the pistol at Ivery's head.

"Don't shoot!" Doc said. "Wait, just wait."

"Are you loco, Doc?" Johnny cried. "Givin' him a gun!"

"Go ahead, Mr. Ivery," Doc replied. "Load the rifle if you can. Load it and shoot your way out of here."

"I can't," Ivery said. "I don't know how."

"He's lying," Johnny cried.

"Pick it up and load it," Raider said, pulling back the hammer on the .44. "Load it or I'll blow your head off."

Ivery began to whimper. He fell to his knees and fumbled with the breech of the Sharps. He didn't know how to cock it. Doc picked up the rifle.

"This poor excuse for a human being couldn't possibly have killed your father," Doc said. "He can't even shoot."

"I don't believe it," Johnny replied.

"Do you think you could have jumped him so easy if he was handy with a gun?" Raider offered. "I think Doc's right, Johnny. This boy didn't kill your pa. Looks like Greeves is our man after all."

"Get to your feet, Ivery," Doc said. "I want you to answer a few questions for me."

"Oh God," Ivery wailed. "I hate this godforsaken place. I never wanted to leave St. Louis. If my sister hadn't . . . Why did I let her bring me?"

"He's somethin' of a weak sister," Raider said.

"Did you help Velma take over the Bar W?" Doc asked.

"Take over?" Ivery replied. "No, we didn't take over. Welton left it to my sister when he died."

"Are you aware that your sister and Judge Greeves conspired to murder Jack Welton?" Doc asked.

"No!" Ivery replied. "It was the Indians that killed him. My sister got a document from the Indian agent."

"Did you see the document?" Doc asked.

"Well, no, but why would she lie to me?"

"Your sister forged Welton's will," Doc replied. "Jack Welton couldn't sign his own name, yet there's a signature on the will in her bedroom."

"The judge helped her," Raider said.

"No!" Ivery cried. "He's our legal representative."

"He wants to take over the Bar W for the cattle and the money he stands to make from the railroad," Raider replied. "Him and your sister are in cahoots, Ivery."

"But why? Why didn't I know?"

"You simply allowed yourself to believe the lies that your sister told you," Doc replied. "However, if you cooperate, you might be given special consideration by the new territorial justice."

"Yes!" he cried. "I'll tell you what you want to know. If I can answer your questions I will. Just don't hang me. Please."

"Ain't nobody gonna string you up," Raider said.

"Tell me," Doc began. "What plans does Greeves have for the Bar W?"

"He plans to take the herd out tomorrow," Ivery replied. "Or at least he's going to let Talbot and his men do it. He's driving them south to Salt Lake City."

"That's all I needed to hear," Johnny said.

Johnny was pointing the Colt toward Raider's head.

"I hate doin' this," Johnny said. "I don't want to drop you, Raider, but I will if you don't give up your gun. I'm takin' Ivery with me right now."

"What's the matter, kid?" Raider replied. "You got maggots for brains or somethin'. Don't be stupid."

"Ivery's my ace in the hole," Johnny said. "He's the only

thing I got to bargain with. Drop it, Raider. You too, Doc. I mean it."

"Let him go, Raider," Doc said.

"I don't like it, Doc. He's gonna get himself killed."

"Do as he says."

Doc tossed the Diamondback onto the ground. Raider relinquished the .44 with a grunt. Johnny pointed to the buffalo rifle.

"I'll take the Sharps, too," Johnny said.

"You're makin' a mistake," Raider said, handing him the rifle. "You kill Ivery and you'll be the one standin' trial for murder, Johnny. Does that make you any better than them?"

Johnny slung the rifle over his shoulder and started backing down the trail.

"I don't want to kill nobody, Raider," Johnny said. "But nobody ain't watchin' out for me in this thing. So I'm gonna watch out for myself. Come after me and I'll kill Ivery and you too if I have to do it. Understand?"

He disappeared into the shadows, dragging a distraught Ivery after him. Raider picked up his .44 and started down the trail. Doc grabbed his arm.

"Don't," he said. "It's getting dark, and even with Ivery in tow, you'd probably never find him."

"I gotta try, Doc."

"Johnny grew up in this valley, Raider. He must know a hundred places to hide."

"Doc . . ."

"And as you said, if he kills Ivery, then he'll have to stand trial for murder. Do you want him to end his life at the end of a rope?"

"No. So what do we do?"

"I was hoping *you'd* tell *me*," Doc replied.

"Hell fire!" Raider cried. "We try to help him, but this damned wet-nosed kid louses it up. He's gonna get himself killed and lose everythin' for bein' so damned pigheaded."

"True," Doc rejoined.

"We should just pack up and get the hell out of here," Raider said. "If he ain't got no more respect than that, he should have to pay for his lack of sense."

"I couldn't agree more," Doc replied. "I take it we're leaving."

"No, we stay, damn it. We wait for morning and see if we can get Johnny out of this mess."

"Why?" Doc asked.

"Hell, ever'body's got their meathooks in Johnny," Raider replied. "We're the only ones on his side. Besides, I like the damned kid, you know what I mean?"

Doc nodded. He knew exactly what Raider meant. He liked the kid too.

CHAPTER FIFTEEN

Raider opened his eyes to the cold, purple half-light of daybreak. As he shivered in his bedroll, he could hear the cattle bawling in the valley below, their mournful sound rising along the ridge like a lament for Johnny's murdered father. He climbed out from under his blanket and peered over the rocks toward the ranch. Even in the semidarkness, he could see that the herd was being driven out of the holding pens.

"Git up, Doc," he said. "It's gonna happen."

Doc rose and shook the confusion from his foggy head. He joined Raider, looking out on the action in the distance. His telescope would be useless until the sun was higher in the east, but he still saw the movement near the holding pens.

"Where the hell is Johnny?" Raider said.

"With any luck, he'll realize the futility of his endeavor," Doc replied.

"When was the last time we had any luck in this thing?" Raider said. "Besides bad luck, I mean."

"Johnny should realize that Ivery will make a better witness than a hostage," Doc replied.

"Maybe," Raider said. "So what the hell can we do?"

They could only watch as the morning sun illuminated

the valley. The herd was a slow-moving entity that crept toward the pass like a colony of black ants on the bumpy plain. The sun was well overhead by the time Doc was able to see Bronc Talbot in his spyglass.

"The big man is riding point," Doc said. "He's in front of the herd. Rather an ugly sort, I'd say."

"He ain't the kind that you'd want to get the drop on you," Raider replied. "Come on, let's move down the ridge and see if we can spot Johnny."

When they were stationed farther north, they could see the pass clearly. Talbot had called back his sentries, apparently to help with the herd. Doc scanned the entire area but still saw no sign of Johnny and his hostage.

"I hope Johnny has come to his senses," Doc said. "After all, what can he do against a small army of men?"

"If he gets in the way, Talbot's gonna squash him like a June bug," Raider rejoined. "Jesus, I hope he don't do nothin' dumb."

Talbot rode out ahead of the herd, approaching the pass with his hand on his pistol. He was looking for Johnny. A banshee howl rolled down the pass with an echo that might have been the Angel of Death. Talbot reined his horse and held a hand over his head.

"There he is," Doc said, pointing toward the other side of the ridge, across the pass.

Johnny stood against the bright sun, holding Sherman Ivery in front of him.

"He's placed the Sharps to Ivery's head," Doc said.

Raider clicked a round into his .30-.30, but it was a futile gesture. He could never cover the kid at such a long range. Johnny cried out again in a frightening cry that reverberated through the pass.

"Talbot! Turn it back or I kill Ivery!"

"Talbot ain't goin' for it," Raider replied.

"Apparently Velma Ivery is giving up her brother as the sacrificial lamb," Doc said. "The herd is still moving."

"Doc, I've got to get across that pass," Raider said.

"How?"

"If I find a narrow place, I can jump it on a horse. If I can get to Johnny before . . ."

"Raider, I don't think . . ."

"Neither do I, Doc. Elseways, why would I want to do somethin' as stupid as I'm about to do."

Before Doc could dissuade him, Raider broke for the horses. He started for the pass in the saddle of a big black gelding. Doc felt helpless as he turned back to the action with his telescope.

Talbot was standing his position as the herd came up behind him. He was glancing to his left, waiting for something. Doc moved his lens around, searching in the direction where Talbot was looking. The glint of a rifle barrel caught Doc's roving eye. He could tell by the bore and the angle of the barrel that a large-caliber rifle was pointed toward Johnny. Talbot's safety valve—Judge Greeves, the old buffalo hunter—was taking aim from below.

"Johnny!" Doc cried. "Run!"

But Doc's voice did not carry to the other side of the pass. He put the glass on the two figures that were dark against the sun. Ivery had gone mad and was screaming out, his voice smaller than Johnny's. As he stepped forward, trying to get away from his captor, the rifle below exploded with a smoky burst. Doc saw Ivery fall, struck in the chest by the slug that had been meant for Johnny. The herd startled at the report of the buffalo rifle.

Doc turned the telescope on Greeves. He saw the black-clad figure rise from the rocks and start for a horse that was tied nearby. Johnny's Sharps erupted in a thundering echo that filled the valley. Greeves fell before he reached his mount. And the herd wheeled around, stampeded by the second rifle shot, rumbling back onto the plain, laying waste to Talbot's men and eveything else in the path of their driving hooves.

Raider's black horse pounded the hard ground to the pass. He arrived at the ledge in time to view the fall of Sherman Ivery and the tumultuous stampede. Across the way, Johnny hovered over the dead body for a moment and then broke for the valley, to finish the judge, Raider thought. Raider's stomach turned over and over as he drew back on the ridge, bolting headlong for the narrow pass, sailing through air, clearing the opening by a couple of feet. He paused only long enough to see that Ivery was gone. Then he started toward the path that led down into the valley, passing Johnny, who could not make as much time on foot.

The gelding flew down the trail, stopping at the rocks in the valley where Greeves had hidden. Raider dismounted and ran to the prostrate figure of the judge. He was lying on the buffalo grass, holding the stump of his leg. Johnny's slug had amputated the limb at the knee. Greeves quivered a few feet away from the severed half of his leg.

"Help me," he moaned.

"I oughta cheat the hangman and let you lay here," Raider said. "It would serve you right."

"Please . . ."

Raider tore off his belt and wrapped it around the stump of the judge's leg, stopping the flow of blood.

"You better thank God that Doc showed me how to make a tourniquet," Raider said.

"You're the one who better start thankin' your Maker," replied a gruff voice.

Raider looked up to see Bronc Talbot.

"How the hell . . . ?"

"I was ridin' in the front," Talbot said. "The stampede didn't git me. Looks like I'm gonna git you, though."

He was staring down the barrel of his pistol, daring Raider to pull on him.

"Try it, asshole!" Talbot growled.

"Do yourself a favor, Talbot. Clear out before my partner gits here."

"I'm takin' the judge with me," Talbot said. "He's my grubstake. He got me into this thing and he's gonna get me out. If he's on my side, I ain't gonna hang."

"You take him and he's gonna die," Raider replied.

"Maybe," Talbot grunted. "But I don't care. If he dies, I pull into Helena with a story about how I almost saved him. Who knows, I might even be the next territorial judge."

He thumbed back the hammer of his pistol.

"Course, I got to pay you back for that whippin' you give me," Talbot said.

"Ain't no need for us to kill each other," Raider replied. "We're both hired guns. If you want the judge, take him. I ain't gonna stand in your way."

"Beggin' for your life, eh?"

"I ain't beggin' for shit, Talbot. But if you shoot me, I'll get one into you before you move an inch. Your men ain't here to back you up now."

"Let's see if you can pull on me with a bullet between your eyes," Talbot replied.

He took aim, prompting Raider's hand to drop. But Raider never got his pistol out of the holster. Johnny's Sharps bellowed again from the rocks behind him. Blood gushed from Talbot's coat. The big man fell with a hole in his chest. A tourniquet wasn't going to save him, Raider thought. Johnny came out from behind the rocks, joining Raider at the fallen figures.

"I'd thank you for my life if you hadn't started all this trouble," Raider said.

"I reckon I finished it, though, didn't I?" Johnny replied.

"Yeah, I reckon you did at that," Raider said. "Come on, help me get the judge on a horse. We gotta meet Doc and finish the rest of this."

"I oughta put another slug in this rifle and make his head disappear," Johnny said.

"You ain't gonna do that," Raider replied.

"What about the woman?" Johnny asked.

"Don't worry, Doc'll think of somethin'," Raider replied. "Come on, we gotta put some fire to that wound or Greeves will bleed to death."

As they put the judge lengthwise on his mount, Johnny was smiling. The cold wind bit his face, but he didn't feel it. He was going home for the first time since his father died. It was a good feeling.

• • •

Velma Ivery was waiting in her bedroom, perched on her fine sofa, dressed in a black high-necked gown that suggested mourning. When Doc entered her chamber, holding his derby in a gentlemanly hand, he saw that Diana Welton was seated a few feet from Velma Ivery, barely conscious of her surroundings. From the glazed look in her eyes, Doc figured that Diana had been drugged.

"Good morning, Mr. Weatherbee," said Velma Ivery. "I'm so glad that you finally arrived. I had feared for my life and the life of my brother. That beast Talbot has held me prisoner in my—"

"Your brother is dead," Doc replied. "So is Talbot."

"Sherman? Oh, no!"

She lifted a black handkerchief to the corner of her tear-less eye.

"My God," she moaned. "I am grief-stricken."

"You've lost your brother to the same man that killed your husband," Doc replied.

"What?"

"Greeves shot your brother with the same buffalo rifle that he used to make you heiress to the Welton ranch," Doc replied. "How convenient that Greeves was here to pull the trigger and sign the fake will."

"I had no choice in the matter," she replied quickly. "They lured me into this scheme. My brother and Greeves. I was against it from the beginning."

"Is that why you tried to convince Jack Welton to become partners with your brother?" Doc offered.

"No, I never—"

"And when he refused, you were happy because you had a reason to kill him then. Wasn't it better to kill him than to have him share your bed every night?"

"Lies!"

"Did you recruit Greeves after Welton refused, or did you bring him in from the beginning?"

"You're fabricating this entire story," she protested. "Besides, with Greeves dead, you can't prove anything."

"You're assuming that we killed him, aren't you?" Doc replied. "The judge is sitting in the bathhouse. I had to burn his wound, but he's going to live. And I daresay he will sing loudly to save himself from the gallows."

"No!" she cried. "I'm innocent! You can't believe his lies."

"Your histrionics will not convince me," Doc replied.

"Perhaps this will," she said, pulling a .25-caliber derringer from the folds of her black gown.

Doc laughed. "If you shoot me, Velma, you won't even have a chance to plead your case to the new territorial justice."

"I'm taking the girl and leaving," she replied. "You won't follow me with her as hostage."

"If you'll look at the window, you'll see that my partner and Johnny are watching us," Doc replied. "If I give the signal, they will shoot you instantly."

"They wouldn't shoot a woman!"

"My partner would relish the chance," Doc replied. "And I needn't remind you of Johnny's thirst for revenge. He has no love for his stepmother. I suggest you hand me the derringer, Miss Ivery."

She hesitated for a moment before tossing him the small pistol. Obviously she held her own life more precious than the others who had fallen in her wake of treachery. A small, knowing laugh escaped from her lips as Doc signaled to Johnny and Raider.

"Do you think they'll hang me?" she asked Doc.

"Given your persuasive powers," he replied. "It wouldn't surprise me if you escaped with your life."

"I never should have underestimated the apothecary," she said.

"My dear," Doc replied. "Your mistake was underestimating a Pinkerton."

EPILOGUE

Doc and Raider stood on the east ridge, peering down at the Elk Lodge Valley and the Bar W. Johnny was trying to round up the herd before the snow came. He had sent word to Bishop's Mill, offering jobs to anyone who wanted to work on the drive to Salt Lake City. One by one stragglers were drifting in, adding to the crew that hurried the scattered herd back into the holding pens. Doc extended his telescope, gazing out over the brownish plain, where first frosts had killed the bitterroot flowers and turned the buffalo grass to a straw color.

"Do you think the drive will get started before snowfall?" Doc asked.

"Yeah," Raider replied. "If I stay and help him, he won't have any problems. He's a good kid and he learns fast. I can show him a few things about cowpunching."

"I didn't know you were a cowpuncher too," Doc said.

"It got me through some rough times when I was a kid," Raider replied. "It's honest, back-breaking work."

"Don't you have to brand the cattle, or something of that nature?" Doc asked.

"Talbot and Ivery took care of that," Raider replied. "Johnny just has to find the strays and move 'em back into the pens. If some of the cows get away, it don't really matter. They got a good chance of surviving the winter.

Might even be a calf or two in the spring if some females get away."

"And speaking of females," Doc replied. "I've sent a telegram to the territorial marshal about our femme fatale and the judge."

"When did you do that?"

"This morning," Doc said. "I found a wire south of here. I suspect that we'll be seeing someone official in a day or two. I'll wait here with the prisoners and accompany them back to Helena. I have to get Judith. What do you intend to do?"

"I think I'm gonna stay here," Raider replied. "Johnny can pay me cowpoke's wages, and I can get the rest of our fee at the end of the drive."

"Good thinking," Doc said. "With the silver mine and the cattle, Johnny will soon be a rich man.

"Besides, the kid is gonna need a good ramrod if he wants to be trail boss."

"Ramrod?" Doc asked.

"He's the troubleshooter for the drive," Raider replied.

"An occupation that you were born for," Doc said.

The wind cut through Raider, chilling his bones.

"Send a wire to Salt Lake City," Raider said. "We'll hook up someplace close to both of us. The boss ain't gonna let us rest too long before he throws somethin' our way again."

"Maybe you'll stumble into another predicament," Doc replied. "If you didn't have a taste for brothels, we never would have met young Welton there."

"Keep it to yourself," Raider growled. "Why the hell did you want to come up to this damned ridge anyway? It's colder'n a well-digger's ass up here."

"It may be some time before we get back this way," Doc replied. "I just wanted to remember this view of the valley. Our Creator's handiwork is something to behold, Raider."

"You know, Doc, you got poetry in you sometimes."

"Why, thank you, Raider."

"I hate poetry," Raider replied. "I'm going to help the kid with the roundup before I freeze to death."

. . .

First snow was falling on Denver. Raider had beat the late October blizzard by a couple of hours, having come down from Salt Lake City after reading Doc's telegram. The snow would make Doc late. He was probably stuck somewhere in that damned wagon, singing to Judith so she wouldn't feel lonely. There was nothing Raider could do about it, so he decided to have supper after he stabled his mount.

In the Delmonico Kitchen, he cleaned a stoneware plate that had been heaped up with steak, onions, and home-fried potatoes. When he was full, he tossed two dollars on the table and strode out into the snowy street. Raider had only been in Denver once before, but he knew a place at the edge of town where a man with a pocketful of money could make a lot of his dreams come true.

"Oh, yes," said a plump woman behind the brothel's bar. "I remember you. The girls talked a blue streak after you left the last time."

Raider tossed a double eagle onto the bar.

"I got to wait for a friend of mine to hit town," Raider said. "How many days will this buy me?"

"You want girls, too?"

"Maybe," Raider replied. "But first I want a bath."

"I can get food from the Kitchen," she said. "You'll have to pay for it. Whiskey, too."

"So how many days for twenty gold ones?"

"Three," she said, smiling with chubby cheeks. "Course, I can't be responsible for the girls. Once word gets around about you, they'll all be wantin' a chance. Includin' me."

Raider winked at her.

"Just keep a runnin' count," he replied.

"Do you remember where the bathroom is?"

"Top of the stairs, right?"

Raider went up to the second floor. The house wasn't as nice as Reva's, but the sheets, the bathwater, and the girls were clean. He found the bathroom and lowered himself into a steaming tub. His body felt lean and tough after the drive. He was damned ready for a woman.

"Want to go to heaven, cowboy?" asked a familiar voice.

Raider turned to see Little Bright Wing standing in the threshold of the bathroom. She was naked beneath a Turkish towel that hid her diminutive frame. Her tiny hands carried a fresh bucket of hot water that she poured into Raider's tub.

"How the hell did you get here?" Raider asked.

"Did you really think Wounded Wolf would keep me on the reservation?" she replied.

"Hell, I guess not," Raider laughed. "You ain't mad at us for giving you back to him?"

"What choice did you have?" she replied. "Bygones are bygones, I can tell you. Besides, you didn't want to give me to him. You spoke up for me."

"Didn't seem human," Raider said. "I guess it don't matter now. You're whorin' again, I see."

"You black-eyed turd!" she cried.

"Get in this tub, girl."

Little Bright Wing dropped the towel and slid over the edge of the tub. Raider felt her soft skin against his legs. Her hands guided him along, and she began to splash gently in the warm water, rising and falling with a smooth, fluid motion. . . .

JAKE LOGAN

___	0-872-16823	**SLOCUM'S CODE**	$1.95
___	0-867-21071	**SLOCUM'S DEBT**	$1.95
___	0-872-16867	**SLOCUM'S FIRE**	$1.95
___	0-872-16856	**SLOCUM'S FLAG**	$1.95
___	0-867-21015	**SLOCUM'S GAMBLE**	$1.95
___	0-867-21090	**SLOCUM'S GOLD**	$1.95
___	0-872-16841	**SLOCUM'S GRAVE**	$1.95
___	0-867-21023	**SLOCUM'S HELL**	$1.95
___	0-872-16764	**SLOCUM'S RAGE**	$1.95
___	0-867-21087	**SLOCUM'S REVENGE**	$1.95
___	0-872-16927	**SLOCUM'S RUN**	$1.95
___	0-872-16936	**SLOCUM'S SLAUGHTER**	$1.95
___	0-867-21163-6	**SLOCUM'S WOMAN**	$2.50
___	0-872-16864	**WHITE HELL**	$1.95
___	0-425-05998-2	**SLOCUM'S DRIVE**	$2.25
___	0-425-06139-6	**THE JACKSON HOLE TROUBLE**	$2.25
___	0-425-06330-5	**NEBRASKA BURNOUT #56**	$2.25
___	07182-0	**SLOCUM AND THE CATTLE QUEEN #57**	$2.75
___	07183-9	**SLOCUM'S WOMEN #58**	$2.50
___	06532-4	**SLOCUM'S COMMAND #59**	$2.25
___	06413-1	**SLOCUM GETS EVEN #60**	$2.50
___	06744-0	**SLOCUM AND THE LOST DUTCHMAN MINE #61**	$2.50
___	06843-9	**HIGH COUNTRY HOLD UP #62**	$2.50
___	07018-2	**BANDIT GOLD**	$2.50
___	06846-3	**GUNS OF THE SOUTH PASS**	$2.50
___	07046-8	**SLOCUM AND THE HATCHET MEN**	$2.50
___	07258-4	**DALLAS MADAM**	$2.50
___	07139-1	**SOUTH OF THE BORDER**	$2.50

Prices may be slightly higher in Canada.

Available at your local bookstore or return this form to:

 BERKLEY
Book Mailing Service
P.O. Box 690, Rockville Centre, NY 11571

Please send me the titles checked above. I enclose _____. Include 75¢ for postage and handling if one book is ordered; 25¢ per book for two or more not to exceed $1.75. California, Illinois, New York and Tennessee residents please add sales tax.

NAME_____

ADDRESS_____

CITY_____ STATE/ZIP_____

(allow six weeks for delivery)

162b